# KURUNCHI
# クルンチ
# குறுஞ்சி

By Steffen Kajendra

## Page of Contents

© 2022, Steffen Kajendra
Forlag: BoD – Books on Demand, Hellerup, Danmark
Tryk: BoD – Books on Demand, Norderstedt, Tyskland
ISBN: 9788743033790

*'My weary feet have become tired.*

*My eyes, looking and looking,*

*have lost their luster.*

*Surely, they are more in numbers*

*than the stars in the wide dark sky,*

*people in this world who are not them.'*

Kurunthokai of Ancient Tamil Sangam Literature : 100 - 300ce

# Identity Lost

Damian and Rachael lay sprawled across the cramped on a low oriental bed, much like spilt milk. Their naked bodies lay extinct, the city on the other hand was bustling, neon lights expressed themselves through the blinds (which Damian had forgotten to close), a monumental Pikachu plastered onto a skyscraper used its height to almost peer into their hotel room. They say if you awaken to the sight of your mother, you will have a great day; Damian woke up believing he may be molested by Pikachu - he knew he was going to have an awful day. He remembered he's in Tokyo. He carefully moved her dead arm which was across his chest as if he were playing Operation and attempted to wipe his drool off Rachael's hair. She doesn't have to know he thought; she will have a shower anyway. Damian's black skin was like moonlight when illuminated by the Pikachu poster on the adjacent building. He watched the city in disgust, turning back to his naked sleeping beauty to contrast his thought of hatred to love. His idea of a trip was not flying half way around the world to eat tasteless sushi, see women painted white doing weird dances and follow preposterous etiquette. Damian came from the nation of Essex you see, his perfect vacation consisted of lying on a beach bed within eye-distance of his five-star Hilton Hotel drinking a Dry Martini with his bikini clad Anglo - Indian girlfriend.

The room was musky with the smell of sex, the completed bottles of Asahi created a Flanking Manoeuvre around the bed, as if to keep them there.
*'Its either this shitty beer or that Kase' shit,'* he mumbled under his voice.
*'Sake',* Rachael's voice was just as musky as the room. Damian watched her rise. Her hair was sticky with drool, to be honest it could have been anything… Her eyes, one stuck by sleep and the other by

forgotten mascara and interlinked upper and lower lashes; she looked fucked. He could not bare to watch her with her make up all ruined , he turned away; for Damian always wanted his woman to look stunning. He was from Essex remember. Damian failed to notice how the yellow light blemished her skin, how her natural beauty had gone way further than whatever she had looked like on any night out. How her lips required nothing artificial, how her untouched (although gross) jet-black hair indicated her Indian heritage.

'What's the time?! We've told the home-stay we will be there for three!',

Rachael was not much of a traveller either, but she hated the rudeness of being unpunctual. Damian looked at her, eyes as hyphen-like as possible, it all came back to him. He was getting no sex today, his nerd younger brother had forced him to visit Mount Koya's Grave of Oda Nobunaga and to prove he had been, a selfie was required in front of the shrine.

Hungover as dog-shit they stumbled hand in hand nowhere. The cab was taking them. Damian wasn't a man of maps or Google Earth for that matter, or else he would've known that it was quicker to walk. The trip itinerary had been texted to him by his brother:

Tokyo - Osaka - Namba station - Gokurakubashi station - Cable car from Paradise Bridge.

Between Osaka and Namba station they were supposed to stop to eat at a home-stay but Damian was having none of it, he did not care about the money he had paid, he refused to stay in someone's home, especially in a place like Asia! Rachael did not put up much of a protest as she wanted to get this over and done with to be back in time for the new season of TOWIE.

*'We will get this done and fly home from Osaka's airport, I'm not staying another day in Japan',* he said while peering down at his map as if it were algebra. When alighting at Gokurakubashi station he finally saw a glimpse of Mount Koya,

*'looks like Snowdonia, just a bit more green'.*

Rachael was not even looking, her interest laid in a crisp packet she could've sworn was Walkers but it said Lays. She was flabbergasted.

Somewhere in Osaka a family waited behind their sliding doors with close to twenty dishes cooked ready for consumption. The children of the family waited excitedly to meet the people staying at their home.

The cable car allowed views boasting of clean-cut Japanese countryside, the level land looked years away from that altitude but no one was watching. When they reached the shrine, a quick selfie was taken. He saw a Shinto priest peering at him and remembered how much of a celebrity he was in Japan because of his skin.
*'I must be the only black guy to have step foot here, this shit is out of the way'.*
Little did Damian know he would not be flying home because of that phrase. Little did he know, he had changed his life forever. The Kannushi turned around in fury,
*'Do you know who built this shrine?'.*
Damian was offended that someone called him out, he was also intrigued that a man in rural Japan could speak English.
*'You are certainly not the first black man here, a man of moonlight built this shrine'.*
Damian was finally interested, Rachael was still thinking about the crisps.
*'Who was he?'*
*'I will tell you when the wind dies down, sit down and have some Sake' for now'.*
Damian sat down, Rachael was checking her snapchat.
He continued, the wind slowed, *'his name was Yasuke - The Black Samurai'.*

## Madrassi and the Monsoon

A hunchback and a broken man watch as the teenager cremates her mother by a river.
Dear Kayal,

This letter is only to be opened when I am gone. I am one of your mother's, the other is India. Born into a land of men, my father gave me to my in-laws in exchange for some land for his cows to graze on. I'm nothing but some land, as is India. I'm a Madrassi, I travelled far with you tied to my chest. From the Andaman's to the Ghats, I took you to unthinkable places. I'm no saint child, I've tried to abandon you; I placed you on a boat and watched it sail. I thought I couldn't bring you up in this man's world. It was too violent, maybe another land might've been nicer to us.
We travelled from village to village dodging rape and scolding women. Countless times I've hung men from palm trees, sick men. Men that deserved to die.

The hunchback is merely a creature stepped on by the same system. Like me and you, he's a Dalit; he means no harm to any of us. The man you call watchman, me and him made you Kayal, but he is no father to you. You know who your parents are. He repents his crimes by forever watching over you, he is broken.

His mother could not give up her land to the next heir. We are just land child. She ordered you and I to be killed. A little babe with a sickle across her neck. My husband had gone off to fight a year before, let's just say; my glistening white saree was blood red as I ran through vibrant jungles in Munnar, Kerala. With you on my back and that same sickle sword in my hand, I ran to the coast. I ran for days. To live in violent lands, we must be barbarians; do you think this fight for us would end in one battle? Thank fuck for the pistol your grandfather left, we owe our lives to it. I was waiting for your father, watching from a rock we call Ela as the Southwest Monsoon bombarded the banana trees.

If there is smoke, my husband is there; the watchman. The rain had discarded the fumes. Where war is, he is. Drenched in Mother Earth I stood at Ela, my red saree soaked, my bindi wiped off, my earrings fighting the windy current; ready to jump. I stood there, eight months pregnant with you and I was ready to rid us both so we may never smell the soil again. That's when it spoke to me, thunder roared, lightning flashed; reflecting off the rain droplets. I could hear her, the cosmos blended around me and all matter shifted into being a physical entity: wind, feeling, anarchy, mystery - it was all tangible.

She said: Millions of women will stand at this spot. Looking out for a man who will never return, watching a land which is not ready for them. They will strive, they will fight. You are not you; you are an embodiment of all the women who have once stood in your place. Not knowing where to go, not knowing whether you will live free or live at all. You will forever be a Mother of India, in a blood red saree watching over the violent cosmos.
We all have our own journey, meet me when you finish yours.

**Kayal folds the paper, she turns to the watchman and the hunchback holding back tears. With her mother burned to ash behind her and the smoke blanketing her eyes:**
**She stands atop a protruding rock in a bright red saree wondering where she will go from here.**
**'*She looks just like her mother,*' said the weeping watchman.**

## Interplanetary Feather of The Natives.

**Here's a story for you fuckers, I am going to kill myself. The colonizers call me Whalley Collins, you'll now know me as Whalley Redhawk.**
**You fuckers will never know. Never. (Flip the page)**

It's been 2186 for three years now since Trump bought time. We have entered a new time, the monetary revolution; from mines in the mantel to the tunnels shooting across the Pacific Desert, we have it all. The wall prevented most of the South Americans getting into America; the ones that survived the flood ventured into the Andes because of the higher ground. We call them Mountain men. They hunt for pelt in the wilderness, they refuse to come down even when the sea had been drunk up. For you see, the Pacific was sold to colonies in Mars, the moon, Io and Titan as converted oxygen from water.
When NASA's curiosity rover on Pluto transmitted images of a pyramid, everyone lost their shit. The Scandinavian union in Greenland instantly decided to send a team there and through the cosmos they travelled for a year (dates and times may differ due to Trump time). Two were sent from America and The Kingdom sent one too.

The Dane stumbled up the grey mountain and looked down into the valley, a black matte pyramid the size of Giza's largest, grasps the green clouds. *'Jesus Christ,'* Michael takes some time to compose himself, *'Are you getting this?'.*
Michael and his crew set up camp and became the first men to sleep on Pluto. He reminded his colleagues to keep on their visors as they would freeze to death otherwise. All night they were plagued with nightmares which in themselves were plagued with screams, cries and endless pain. They waited for the Americans to arrive, the longer

they waited the more intense the nightmares got; one morning Michael woke up to a feather drawn on the inside of his space helmet. They fled from the pyramid, building a camp five miles South of Black Rock. That night Michael dreamt of the death of his babies and the rape of his wife. She smiled and looked straight into his eyes as it took place. He woke up gasping for air and peered out of his gold covered tent. Rasmussen (the youngest of the four men crew) lay dead bearing a switch-blade slashed across his neck.

When the Americans arrived, the Danes lay dead sprawled across the tough grey land. One of the tents shook, upon unzipping Michael was found shivering in fear sleeping next to a dream-catcher. Following a warm cup of brew and some celestial crackers he warned them,

*'get the 3D printer to make you dream catchers, they seem to work.'*

No -one dreamt. Michael loaded the dead onto the craft for their journey home whilst the Americans explored the structure. Ancient inscriptions laced the monument on every level. The calligraphy shimmering in gold against the black background was decimated as the American worked his way through with a chainsaw, a piece falls clean off. The Americans scurry off with the piece just as the drone finishes its aerial shots across the structure. It was time for home.

The second US party and the Kingdom's team aborted mission as they passed by Jupiter, Pluto was warming and had become gaseous once again. They wondered where the pyramid would fall. The grey surface withered in cosmic mist slowly rising into gas, the pyramid was blessed with a plethora of green and violet vapour which encompassed across the Great Planes of Pluto. By the time Michael's party of the dead arrived back on Earth with the American's, the year was still 2186.

President Trump Jr called for a conference to understand the meaning of this pyramid. A bear symbol was inscribed on the piece which was taken off, Trump watched in awe.

*'It's Native American,'* the council member of the Mountain Men walked out as he said it,

*'If any Arikara remain, they may be able to read it'.*

Trump ordered the man to stay, the man smirked.

The Scandinavian community found it hilariously ironic that the answer to interstellar travel lay within the American soil, not even a sign to indicate their graves. Native American space men. How much can a civilization learn from being isolated for ten thousand years? The Scandinavians convinced the world that this was an American investigation, they fucked up so they fix it; and with that the search had begun for the last Ree.

(Flips page)
**I bleed for my ancestors, our secrets will die with the wind. Nature and natives complement one another, every tree felled, every river dried - my people were thought to watch from nether planes, little did they know - they were watching from the stars. Do I want to know what it means? I'm sure I will find out. By Redhawk.**

The soldiers surrounding the house watched in horror, blood flowed from Whalley's temple.
At the next conference Trump read the note, in a fit of fury he threw it across the room.
'What do we do now?'
'Who else can read it?'
Scandinavian council members erupted into a fit of laughter and the Mountain Man sat with a wide grin planted across his face.

## Love's Time's Beggar


For even a single hour sprints past when they would talk. Wide eyed, he would stare when she told her stories. When did money matter? Time? They both hung onto each-other suspended in a vacuum, void of time, touch and space. Just bopping.
But Love's time's beggar.

Love is the idea of truly sharing your life with someone. The idea that there's someone that knows everything about you, what side you sleep on, your smell, your thought process, how you deal with pimples. Since childhood we've been taught to share, and when you finally share love there is no better feeling. So much so that we beg for more time.

A candle flickers brightest in the darkness but it too is subservient to time. It withers and wafts off - mistakes are made, words are ejected, hate is pushed from one side to the other. Both scurry to their own corners going through what they go through. Wide- eyed he would watch you as you spoke, now enraged he glares into nothingness thinking about who she's with and you stare out to the horizon wondering who he is with. Not knowing that the idiots are with each-other. Just on an alternate plane.

Meetings do occur, powered by alcohol they either fight or they kiss but they never really talk. The kisses end in fights and the fights end in sadness. *'He would never speak to me like that'*, is what is thought when the dust settles. Another meeting, pure hatred is spat at each-other; *'I hate you and I don't care about you'*, the forthcoming silence lasts ten seconds, time now sloth's onward. Why does everything hateful have to last so long?

Now boy and girl both sit, eyes and ears are not vigilant to anything other than the voice of their heart which only speaks love. For hate is a form of love, a twisted form of love wherein an accumulation of pain, love and betrayal explodes in the face of your significant other. The yellow light, it may be gone but the wick is still hot, orange tints are still visible amongst the black soot. One must care enough to hate.

Boy sits and questions everything he's done. Girl questions whether she did anything wrong in the relationship. Hate the one you love but don't forget you love them.

Here lies the death of a relationship. Ten others died around the globe in this hour. Time took its toll.

## Lost Love

Emily was at work, she'd started to think about all the men she let in. She went through them, all fifteen of them and had realised that maybe five were genuine. The three others that she couldn't remember were somewhere in her phone. She types away at the computer. Across the office, her friend Sandra and her partner Jess discuss paperwork complications.

Sandra and Jess live in a cramped one bed studio in the city. Cluttered with dream catchers, energy stones and singing bowls. Through adultery, mayhem and misunderstandings; they still pulled through. In the night, Sandra would read Keats and Wordsworth aloud to their lovebirds as if to play Beethoven to a deaf man.
*"These creatures understand the language of poetry. All creatures do, look how their eyes flicker at the end of each verse"*, she would say.
Then Jess would realise, every night she falls for the same woman. It feels eternal.

Anyway, when Emily found Lenin she started to think about how he was an amalgamation of what all the other men had lacked. Niceness, care, intrigue and wonder. She didn't understand it, her initial reaction was a failure to trust anything Lenin spoke of from then on. You see there was no reason to,
*'All men are after one thing, they're trash,'* her single friends would say and they were right. What she wanted sat opposite her, sipping a dark cup of coffee, eyes painted paradise blue - her experiences barricaded her view. All she saw were those men.
She started to nitpick.

Lenin had returned from a spiritual awakening in Costa Rica, UNICEF allowed him to see the true world in its entirety- the pain people go through for a bowl of rice, suicides that occur between starry eyed inter-caste couples. His philosophy of life was this: before you're gay, straight, transexual, black, white or pansexual; you're a human of Earth and should be treated as such. He wondered why she picked at him, but nevertheless he understood her beauty and the beauty in her flaws.

Months had passed, Lenin and Emily were official. The nicer the things he did, the further Emily was drawn away. Her friends, like her, were apprehensive. The night they made love, Lenin lost his virginity, he didn't sleep that night. He saw nothing, no existential crisis, no world hunger, no war or poverty; all he saw was Emily's face. Milk coloured, silk textured, rose pink blemished skin. Her nose twitched with a cute redness at the tip, it was cold in that room.

When she told him that they were finished a week later. He questioned it angrily, he was told he was volatile and she didn't feel safe. The question ran through his head, the whiskey drained out of the cup, the cigarettes smoked till his tonsils dried, the eyes twitched, the soul pained, the mind wandered, but love bulged. His friend Alan advised him, *'be more like me, just use them. How are you catching feelings?'*. As the Jack Daniels finished so did his epiphany, the pure act of niceness had got him here. If he didn't care for people of Earth, if he didn't give a shit, if he did it for the sex there would be no pain entrenched within him. He would be a new man.

In the wet streets of the Aarhus, with the street-lights singing songs of light. Knocking back a glass of wine Emily looks to her friends. Behind her act, she misses Lenin. Her friend refills her glass of wine, *'men ain't shit'*, she says. Panning out from the club, below the looming dormant cloud Lenin lights a joint. After passing the joint to Alan, he turns away hiding a single tear. Alan puffs at it, loving the new strain as he says *'women ain't shit man'*.

**The city cries in the dark as the grey cloud explodes billions of droplets.**

<u>Yasuke' - The Mute Child</u>

Two Children, One Man.

**1554 – Mozambique, Lake Malawi**

Issufo's father, much like other members of the Yao Tribe, left his village to live in his wife's village. By Lake Malawi, the breeze at dawn was a spectacle to see; the storks fishing for their young, crocodiles bathing with their families in the sun, cheetahs cooling themselves in the branches of tall trees further up the cliffs, elephants splashing about in the water, Issufo playing cat and mouse with his parents. He falls over. Both his parents run to his aid and blow on the scratch on his knee.

Women controlled the society, men were tasked with going out hunting whilst the Chieftess' would tend to more political matters. Issufo would sit on Chieftess Heda's lap playing with the straws protruding from her elaborate outfit.. Being rocked by the beloved leader, he playfully smiled across to his mother who smiled back; her smile illuminated the engravings on her dark skin, her smile stretched from one side of her face to the other and her eyes glistened like Lake Malawi did before the sun receded back to its realm. It was the last time he would see his mother's smile.

Under the Baobab tree, Heda questioned the unusual man who had come seeking a proposal at the village. All the women stood around the man, one woman passed around her deer antler water pipe as

the man spoke: 'please, just listen to what I have to say, times are changing – the old gods do nothing for your illnesses,'.
Heda retorted with *'ah, a religion of peace, but we are already peaceful, it will make no difference, but can I ask, why the circumcision? I don't want to hurt our little ones.'* The man responded with his argument, explaining that the pain was momentary and questioned why the women would engrave themselves if it was painful. Chieftess Heda had no answer.

Under Issufo's straw outfit he was terrified, he didn't understand the procedure that was going to take place.
*'You're a brave little boy Issufo, lead the other children',* said his mother with her head placed onto his. Issufo trotted into the hut and was told to lie down, when the man took an instrument out, Issufo saw something sharp through the straw and darted across the hut, out into the tall, green grass. He kept running, running through the elephant grass, as far as his little feet would take him. He couldn't really see where, but he ran. He reached a cliff edge and fell into the Lake, the current took little Issufo downstream, he floated in his straw outfit.
The villagers searched for days.


### 1555 – North Eastern Ethiopia, Dalol, Danakil Depression

*'Yasufé, throw me my sword!',* shouted his father from across the bush. Yasufé panicked, his little hands scurried through the crimson dust, he picked up the sword and threw it across to his father. The hippopotamus skin making up the handle scraped his finger as he did so, he began to bleed from his hand. At the tender age of six, his life was going to end; written out of the mists of time. He turned to the mauled corpse to his left, what was once his mother lay ripped to shreds. The thread he tugged at by his mother's hip as his little feet would follow her around had been torn clean off. He wrapped it around his little wrist and lay next to his mother in a foetal position sucking his thumb weeping.

Not a cloud in the sky, the Ethiopian heat scorched the plains, rocks cracked in the boiling air. The natural chemicals surrounding the hot springs created a wave of colours: shades of green, blue, yellow and orange – which reflected off his fathers two sickle swords. One in each hand with the base of the swords at stomach level, Yasufé watched as his father stood against three lions like the king he was. The lions were most likely descendants of ones which had escaped the Roman Empire, for they behaved like gladiatorial creatures; more ferocious than nature intended.

He peered over his mothers twitching corpse, his father lashed out his right arm, slicing a cat's throat; blood gushed down onto the dirt and ran through the Earth. He dropped the sword, with the same right arm as he reached for his club which was tied to his right knee, he caught the other beast's jaw with ferocious power. The dislocation of that creature's jaw echoed across the plains and so did its whimpers as it lay on the ground, for it was merely hungry but now it was beaten, dying. The third lion pounced onto his father, ripping a new hole into his throat every chance it got, similarly the warrior sliced at the lion's stomach repeatedly. Yasufe lay back with his mother, he could not watch his father's dying light, nor could he continue watching this massacre.

Lying in a pool of dried blood, surrounded by three dead lions and his two dead parents, Yasufé, the little child lay motionless.

Days later, a party of mule herders shoo away the vultures and flies to scavenge the corpses and skin the lions for hide.
*'This quality of this hide is awful, it's got holes everywhere',* said the older gentleman. The men stripped Yasufé's body for clothing, but when one of them placed a hand on a red thread laced across his arm, Yasufé covered it with his other arm.

The men were astonished, 'Who is this child?'.

**1563 – Mombasa Coast, Kenya**

Alessandro Valignano, a Portuguese Jesuit missionary walked up and down a line of black men, chained by their ankles. In the middle stands a man, a man with skin like moonlight, a jaw stronger than Mount Kili of Tanzania, arms defined to perfection. The man had a fierce look in his eyes, although chained; this man looked free.
*'Your name?',* questioned Valignano.
There was no response.
*'Very well, I will name you Izaque; after a patriarch from the Book of Genesis'.*
And with that, they set sail on an old missionary ship which now transported pilgrims, travellers and people running away from their past. He sat and watched the other passengers, he clenched the thread on his arm and kept his straw hat close to him. Izaque did not know where he was going, but he took pleasure in looking at a woman dressed in a red saree. On her back was a sickle sword and shield, she turned over to Izaque and smiled. Her bindi was exotic to him, he smiled back – she looked like his mother.'

### 1579 – Off the Coast of Japan
Izaque peered out to the landmass. Japan. He was excited to help Alessandro convert this nation to Christianity. Alessandro Valignano watched Izaque's eyes glisten, he could never have known what would become of Yasuke.

### 2019 - Mount Koya, Japan

**Damian and Rachel sat, wide eyed – gulping down at the Saké as the Kannushi continued the tale of Yasuke – The Black Samurai.**

## Waves From The South.

*What is my mother to yours?*
*How is my father related to yours?*
*Although you and I knew not each-other in any way,*
*Just as red earth and pouring rain:*
*The love-filled hearts merged.*
 - **Kuruntokai, Sangam Literature - 40./400BC +**

**750 BC Age of Second Gathering - South of Madras, Tip of Sri Lanka.**

In Sanskrit it was known as the Sangam, ancients called it the Koodal or The Gathering. Scholars, gods and goddesses went as pilgrims to the sacred Temple of Seven Pillars to pay homage to the Great Lord Shiva. He himself was said to attend with the defiant Kali whom Shiva (throughout eternity) would calm. Many Sangam's ago, in the age of the gods, ancient Shudras drowned the footsteps of Shiva in molten gold which over time solidified. They were then quickly beheaded as a peasant may not metaphorically or physically attempt to reach or touch the air surrounding such divine feet.

For millennia, tradition, as a cliff face to coastal tides, stayed stagnant for The Gathering would occur twice a year by the converging oceans to the South. Outside Sangam meetings, scholars and esteemed writers scoured India and Sri Lanka in search for all culturally important texts. Compiled pieces were read aloud at The Gathering, they were analysed by legends of art - esteemed poets of the Old Pandya Dynasty, four hundred of them to be exact, who would decide upon which works were incorporated into the famous anthologies of the Sangam. All texts fell under the 'puram' rule, meaning outer field, which was used to portray public values: wars, scenery, Hinduism and Jainism.

I

**Beautifully** chocolate, was the skin of the old, blind woman dehulling lentils with a pestle and mortar. Beedi smoking men conversed about their new stitched sarongs as the woman walked by with her fresh catch of the day. Giant fish-heads protruded from the clay walls of her hut, as if to peer down at her washing the fish one more time before cooking commenced. Ilyae could be heard praying next door, the woman wondered why her prayers were so deafening on this particular day.

*'Ilyae, shut your mouth. I can't even be lonely in peace,'* shouted the woman as she stormed into Ilyae's hut.

*'The Sangam is here, do you think they're pleased with my prayers? I pray to Shiva just for them',* replied Ilyae.

'To hell with your prayers, pray for yourself woman, pray that this fish cooks itself'.

When Midday crept over the Ghats, the fish curry was complete and the woman inked drawings of fish, wrote ballads of her hardships and recipes onto dried seaweed. She started this venture after she caught her first squid. She could not concentrate. For the origins of the ruckus had transferred from Ilyae's prayers to the squabbling poets nearby.

Armed with her book, she left her hut in a white saree covered in dirt with dried seaweed hanging from the thatched roof wafting in the breeze behind her. She turned to the smokers,

*'I can't concentrate boys',* she paused and asked herself why she thought they could help her. She yanked the beedi from the man closest to her and walked off wielding a book in one hand and the smoke in the other with a yellow bindi streaked across her forehead… Towards The Gathering she paced.

Poets sat on long graphite benches which curved around for metres on end forming a semi – circular complex akin to a Roman circus split in half. In the middle, a graphite platform which was surrounded by the golden dust of the land. In the centre, surrounded by a couple hundred members of the Gathering lay the sacred golden footsteps which glistened in the Indian sun. The reflection hid in her eyes, blinding her as she confidently marched up to the platform.

*'I would like to submit a piece'*, she yelled.
A member of the Gathering, Uru saw but ignored completely. He was the head of the Sangam. The lands by the coast were painted with dots of brown dressed in white silk, shimmers from the sun enlightened the beauties of the land – the tall trees in the forests to the North, the red earth surrounding the Jaffna settlement, little silver anklets bouncing across the beaches, the mammoth Sigiriya reaching out to the heavens and the waves edging in from the South. Lord Shiva's view from the skies must have been cosmic, if the Great Pharaoh Khufu were atop of the pyramids, he still would have been envious, as would the Harappan Kings towards Andhra, for the country between the Ghats and the Indian Ocean was nature's secret, its secret box of beauty.

*'I WOULD LIKE IT IF I COULD SUBMIT MY PIECE',* she screamed.
Uru turned to her with a stern look.
*'This is the Koodal, you are not permitted here. You must address us as members of the Gathering. You will not come here and scream,'* he demanded as he turned to continue his conversation with another member.
*'So why do you make so much noise? I cannot think in the village and I tire from being out at sea,'* her voice had quietened down.
*'If this is all you require, we will speak somewhat quieter. If your actions create a detrimental environment in which we know not what books to publish – your head will roll. Now be gone.*
*'I would like to submit a piece,'* she reached for her book of seaweed as she expelled smoke from her chapped lips.
*'Who even are you, where do you inherit such disrespect? Does your book consider the land, Velir or Pandya dynasties? Does it teach us to further write our own texts?'*
Uru was growing increasingly angry.
*'It is about me.'*

The Gathering erupted into laughter as Uru instructed a Pandya warrior to expel her from the Sangam.

Her head smacked against the hard-dusty floor, her knees bled profusely, and tears rolled down her cheeks, she rested the back of her head on the ground as she turned over to question the skies. She thought maybe she would catch a glimpse of Lord Shiva dancing in the skies. She saw nothing.
A streak of blood polluted the purity of the white cloth. Ilyae dragged the dazed woman, her feet slid along the earth; her friend scolded her repeatedly.

By the golden feet of Shiva, the seaweed pages of her book turn with the wind. Up in the Ghats, a bearded man sits amongst a swaying storm and watches over the land, smiling.

The villagers watched as their neighbour is led back home, the old woman (now washing her lentils) laughs to herself:
*'Little girl,'* she begins to herself, *'in a straw canoe tied to a coconut with a name: Girl. A young mother somewhere, part of some dynasty. Said to have been raped by a warrior of another dynasty and thus with Kaali's fury she takes her own life out of shame after she lets the girl flow down the river - Kaveri. This child is all grown up now. Her writing is Akam – writings of the soul. It's just the wrong time…'*

The Sangam would inherit texts of Akam – the inner field. Akam and Puram transformed writings of the land to carry both the soul and nature. Several hundred years would pass before this though, creating a school of writing for all people, not only the top castes. What exists in one's mind exists for all, what is not understood; will be, in time. The woman was uncredited for introducing this type of text and so for countless monsoons; she would go out to sea and return with fresh fish.

The blood had left a stain, one day she stood up from her boat to peer over at Sri Lanka from India. She was uncertain.

The stone bridge between the countries crumbles from the
crashing Waves from the South.

A Passage from The Diary of Alessandro Valignano
(1) For God's Sake'
Date: June – 1582

Road from Kashima, province of Portuguese Nagasaki.

Dear Diary,

Letters came from all corners of Japan at the same speed which
Alexander pursued Darius through Asia centuries ago. Even the
horses seemed to sigh every time a peasant ran towards our
company screaming 'Nanban! Nanban!'

The most recent messenger came running, fanning himself
vigorously, at the top of his voice he expelled, *'Oda Nobunaga – the
great unifier and Daimyo of all of Honshu has died!'*. My trusted
samurai – Muso Gonnosuke drew his katana as the peasant started
to pray, he had just noticed my attendance. A speck of blood
sprinkled onto the bowl of rice that I was to consume, and the
peasant lay headless on the sun-soaked land. I shouted at
Gonnosuke, I implored that he may be a ronin, but a serving samurai
who must adhere to orders and so I questioned his actions.

He began as he always does *'Forgiveness Padre…'* Gonnosuke's
voice was stern but inherited a respectful tone. In confidence, the
young samurai declared that the peasant should be honoured to die
from a clean sweep under the sharp steel of his katana as he had
disrespected both himself and me. Gonnosuke understood that the

peasant had no formal education, but he cannot fan himself with a sensu embellished with a golden handle. At most, he is to use a full wooden sensu or uchiwa.

I offered the bowl of rice to Gonnosuke who proudly refused, and I thought about the land. Daimyo controlled the region and the Shogunate controlled the Emperor who thought they controlled the Daimyo. I called it pagan barbarism when I set foot on this soil but how different are they to priests, the bank and the Roman church. One thinking it controls the other. I can't utter such words.

**June 22 1582,**

Dear Diary,

It is true, Oda Nobunaga is dead. In retaliation, Hideyoshi and Nobunaga's third born: Oda Nobutaka ride out to Kyoto bloodthirsty for traitor Mitsuhide's bloodline. On this long road to Nagasaki, the sea breeze sends droplets in the direction of my trusted samurai; they don't seem to enjoy a salty mouth. We move passed Kashima, two letters arrived.

One from Rome, the church insists that Portuguese Nagasaki is not to be utilised for economic advantages. How else would I fund the conversion of Shinto priests to Men of the Church? How would I feed the practicing Padre? How do I print posters spreading the word of Christ? Who commissions the building of idols, churches and accommodation for the Portuguese? I threw the notice on the ground.

The other from Nagasaki, The Woman in Red demands my attendance. How dare she demand anything from me? I own Nagasaki. Gonnosuke reminded me who she was, I had seen her once, some years ago. She is not someone to lock-horns with; I guess I must see her straight away.

I don't care for feudal barbarism or women of the Indus. I look over towards billowing smoke from this little village by the sea – my mind goes to Izaque. Oda is dead, but what of the servant? The boy. The boy I helped raise.

## Aappu and the Deformed Child

*'More unfathomable than the waters*
*Is this love for this man*
*Of the mountain slopes*
*Where bees make rich honey*
*From the flowers of the Kurunci*
*Which has such black stalks'* - **Kuruntokai of the Sangam
Literature 400BC - 40BC.**

### Context

**1920's in Jaffna, British Ceylon and the Villages surrounding it.**

By the tip of the Northern flat lands of British Ceylon lies the second largest city in the country, Jaffna City which is controlled by Sir William Henry Manning. He would travel the length of the Commonwealth delegating administration powers to Edward Stubbs who would actively go on to oppose the poor Sinhalese workers in the plantation fields up in the cloudy mountains of Middle Ceylon for which he would resign in the 30's. With colonial leadership such as this, indigenous peoples were treated like dogs if they were poor. For the Tamils up in the flat North, the domination was a little more bearable; these ancient people enjoyed the tranquillity of their lush villages as they dodged the odd Christian conversion.

## Chapter One

### Kandaa Village, 13km from Jaffna's Centre

A heavily pregnant Geetha clad in a white cotton cloth draped as a sari with a similarly dirty skirt trots around the village as she pushes her arm into her back whilst also adjusting her blouse.
*'Nice and cool out today don't you think?'* She yelled out to a slow but occupied village.
Her call gathered all ears, including cockerels hidden under large straw bowls. The sound diffused through the houses as they were situated between the smallest pockets of jungle. This meant that the homes carried their own micro - ecosystems bordered from their neighbours by several banana and palm trees. The red earth meandered through the barriers of nature as a snake would, and by the head of this snake sat several elders in sarongs squatting under the windless skies drinking their palm wine.

The children came running from the main road from where they were able to see a rare motor car or brush horses which stopped by the nearby tea shack. They passed by Geetha as they ran from the road and disappeared into the fauna. The coachman chased them wielding the stick that the kids had used to make the horse sneeze, and as his sarong slipped from his waist, he dropped the stick and nervously laughed to the villagers before returning to his cart.

*'It is mighty refreshing today, it's warmer indoors!',* shouted Lekha who was in the shower. Dried palm leaves thatched vertically made up the walls of her shower room. The sun kissed her fourteen year old dark skin. Lekha lived opposite Geetha's home with her two little sisters, mother Panchu and her father, who rested in a colourful clay

pot in the form of ash. Lekha would sit with her as she read stories from the weekly printed magazines that came down the road from Jaffna. The last article was about why garlic is bad for you. This would be until the jealous Panchu, whose large size and hanging assets would wobble as a shadow across the dusty path and pull Lekha back home, by the hair.

*'The night is no place for a girl,'* she would shout.

*'But I want to learn!'.*

*'Female children have nothing to learn, just stay in the hut and preserve yourself. Maybe you might make a good mate for someone,'* Panchu muttered as they disappeared back into their hut.

Panchu's problem with Geetha was as old as her marriage. Panchu's husband was a fisherman, he had worked with Aappu for years. Aappu then went on to study in Jaffna's Central College as his Geeta would face poverty back at home. She ate at Panchu's home and was even nursed by her. Several years later Aappu graduated in Architecture and began his work for the colonials. It was during this time that Panchu's husband contracted HIV from a girl in a passing theatre troupe. He then died of an ear infection. Panchu blamed the evil eye she had been subjected to by Geetha and proclaimed that Aappu was a traitor and a pawn for the whites. She sat in front of one of the village's two sacred statues - the one of Shiva and cried till her brother dragged her and little Lekha away vowing to finance their life. Panchu would always lament on how her husband was a lion but she then somehow had two more children after his death. No one questioned this.

*'Dont scrub yourself too hard, you might turn white!'* called out Geetha as she waddled around with her hands still perched onto her back.

*'But that is what I want!'* Lekha yelled back.

Panchu then quickly entered the frame, taking up most of it; she said *'Geetha, why don't you head back inside till your husband returns. Aappu wouldn't want you out in the view of all these men',* she juggled paan in her mouth and looked in the direction of the old men. One of them was swatting a mosquito.

*'At least mine will return. You bored yours to death!'* shouted Geetha with her six month embryo determining her savage emotions.

Panchu ran over to Geetha wielding a sickle sword used to crack coconuts and roared profanities at her. Lekha who was bathing herself from top to bottom rolled her eyes because she knew it was just another day in Kandaa. *'Slut, whore, dancer...'* All these terms were heard. The kids behind the palm trees giggled and repeated them like parrots. In a fit of fury, Panchu accidentally kicked the straw bowl over to reveal all of Geetha's hens and chicks dead. They both froze in horror as a lizard scuttled around the outer wall of her home. They peered down and saw a snake curled up around a dying chick. Geetha reached for the sickle sword from Panchu's frozen body and hacked the snake to death. The village fell silent and brown faces peered into her front yard. At this exact time, in the shower; Lekha noticed that there was blood between her legs and called out to her mother.

## Chapter Two

### Jaffna City. Around the same time.

Hammers fractured the dry red earth around the tracks. The land had been thawed out to provide the foundation for the new buildings. British soldiers trotted about on their horses with papers and binoculars.

*'My village is about thirteen kilometers down that road'*, pointed Aappu to his two colleagues who were draped in dust.

*'Boys you must come, my wife is having our first child in a few months. You guys can meet him!'*. He exhaled heavily, *'I work so hard by these tracks that I am starting to think they lead to her.'*

His co-workers looked at him and then turned to the British officers walking above them, both of them proceeded to scratch their heads and walk off.

The smile on Aappu's face refused to wash off, he turned and pointed his arm out to another man behind him for a handshake: *'Your name?'* he asked confidently.

*'Ruwan Weerawansa,'* replied the Sinhalese man who caught his hand above the parched earth.

Without a pause Ruwan said:

*'What makes you think they will let you see your wife?'*

At first Aappu's expression almost transformed to a concerned one.

*"By the centre is St Mary's. Do you know why there are no buildings behind it? That is where they buried them, my friend. Workers like you… In denial. "*

To which Aappu hastily interrupted with:

*'I am not like those other boys, I come from a generation of farmers; it's all in the records. I am here to help oversee the project as a building planner'.*
Ruwan was not convinced at all, he took a good look at Aappu. He did not look educated. This man was dressed as a Dalit, a small piece of cloth covered his genitals and buttocks which was held up by a string, a cloth bound together on his head formed his white turban and white streaks of sacred ash brushed across his forehead. The afternoon sun moisturised his skin causing pebbles of sweat to disintegrate into the red, hot sand.
Aappu - the naked village man, called out to Officer McShea.
*'Where is Officer Rudyard?'* asked Aappu as if he were speaking to an old friend.
*'In some shithole somewhere looking for something',* replied the young Mancunian.

Ruwan's jaw hung as low as his sarong.


Thirteen kilometres away, Officer Skip Rudyard wanted to ride to Kandaa, he wanted to see the surroundings roll across the Sri Lankan plain but Joseph Charles, a Sri Lankan born missionary and unwanted companion, refused. The first time Joseph met Officer Rudyard, he began as he always does:
*'Hello Mr Officer, my name is Josep Charles,'*
To which the old serviceman erupted into laughter under his thick white moustache. His inability to make the 'ph' sound meant that he wasn't able to say his own name and so Skip called him Jeppy and would make him say words such as philanthropy.
Meanwhile in the jungle, surrounded by thatched roofs and Jack fruit trees Geetha and Panchu burnt the snake in full view of the young ones of the village. The drunken elders cursed Geetha for killing a sacred Naga. She was told to repent by praying to the other statue in town - the Manasa goddess who was idolized as a deity by the ones that settled in Kandaa a few generations ago. Geetha refused. Manasa, the snake goddess and daughter of Shiva was unforgiving and possessed the ability to bound one to eternal darkness, even throughout future reincarnations.

As the women walked down the dusty path to their homes, they discussed Lekha's puberty ceremony.

*'Well I guess we need to find her a husband after the ceremony, how old were you when you married again?'* Asked Panchu who was trying to remember.

*'I was twenty one'.*

*'I was thirteen',* interrupted Panchu as she giggled, continuing:

*'See, you married late; that is why you've had no children for so long. It has been what? Twelve years?'*

Geetha's head stooped low, she looked down at her yellow wedding strand and thought out loud,

*'I studied for two years.'*

Panchu expelled a cackling song of laughter which shook the combined mass of her existence,

*'studied? For what?'*

Geetha shrugged her shoulders and resumed her waddle.

Closer to their homes by a sleeping stray dog lay an old Kuravar. Lekha peeked through some vegetation at the old man.

*'Fucks sake its him again, I'm running away'* whispered Panchu as she scuttled off. Geetha stood over the old peasant, the bump blocked most of the man's view. She was unafraid, and she knew about the Kuravar. She knew about their exploits from their tribal home up in the Western Ghats of South India but she did not know how he had crossed the Palk Strait between India and Sri Lanka without the British spotting him. She also knew how to use these ancient gypsies, Aappu had taught her all about them. One could ask them for the local news, to read your palm or even for ayurvedic medicine, however she was also told not to be alone with one. They had been known to be cannibalistic.

*' From the Himalayas to the Maldives. I have been everywhere. What do you need from me girl',* he expelled as he lit his beedee.

*'Old Kuravan. Tell me the story of my village today,'* she yelled aloud as to test his hearing.

*'Two officers cart in on wheels from the city. They wish for you to love Christ,'* he responded, puffing out smoke, never once opening his eyes.

*'Fuck, fuck, fuck!*, she shrieked as she ran to Panchu's hut.

## Chapter Three - The Banana Leaf Principle

*' Jeppy, is this your first time doing missionary work in your own country?'* questioned Officer Rudyard.

*'Yes sir, but I have worked in Kenya and Abyssinia,'* Jeppy paused, sensing uncertainty and said *'But truth is easy to spread wherever you are sir'*.

Skip looked Jeppy up and down, his eyes rested upon Joseph's black clerical shirt. He was even wearing a soft white cloth inserted into his tab collar to seem as a priest would.

*'Are you even qualified to wear that?'*

*'Of course sir, I have certificate,'* answered Jeppy confidently.

*'As a priest?'* Skip pushed a little.

*'Yes of course sir,'* came another rapid Jeppy response.

*'Then why are you married?'*

Silence occupied the cart. For several minutes, the dark skin of the missionary dripped with perspiration. He adjusted his attire but was only able to look more ridiculous since the tightness of his shirt pushed out his cheeks which conquered the majority of his face.

Skip started again: *'Look Jep, we use something with the Hindu's here called The Banana Leaf Principle.'*

He started to explain in the most robotic way, he was tired of having to explain this. *'A Hindu eats rice and curry on a banana leaf, not plates like us. We have to see whether they have banana trees or chopped leaves left out to dry. Once we have confirmed this, we can work on converting them.'*

Geetha called out to all the kids of the village and told them that missionaries were on their way. From this point, the village kicked into action, Kandaa had transformed its lazy demeanour into a bustling operation. The adolescent girls removed anklets from their legs, the boys all ran to the fields to work, the little children removed their Shaivite bracelets, the women gathered over the well to wipe off their bindi's followed by the old men whom scrubbed sacred ash from themselves. Both the holy statues had been stripped of all their ash, gold and ribbons of worship to cunningly represent neglect. Once all of this was over, the village split into four due to the village having only four cows, one by one the cows were overfed banana leaves until Kandaa was undressed of all Hinduism. An almost transparent aura of dust was still bouncing over the straw huts when Officer Rudyard and Jeppy came along.

Joseph walked around the village with his eagle eyes equipped. He assessed and analysed the fauna and would run over to random trees. The officer issued Bibles to all the men in their huts, the women were told to run away out of fear of rape so they were nowhere to be seen. Panchu and Geetha however stayed put inside the former's hut after telling Lekha to look after her smaller siblings in the fields. Just then, the dried wood functioning as a door started to shake.

Geetha trotted out of the hut and bent her neck back to look up at Skip. He began to point at Panchu's banana tree and say something in a foreign tongue. Geetha was fascinated by his white, silky skin; and so she reached for his arm and tried to rub his skin. It did not come off. The prickly old officer was quite amused, he just watched the intrigue in the dark, pregnant girl's eyes. He noticed her suspended tear-drop earrings before anything else. Then came her small forehead which led into the darkest black hair he had ever seen. Her giant eyes differed from her very small lips which reminded him of his very own daughter back in Cornwall.
*'English?'* she whispered.
Skip was in shock. He nodded.
*'What the fuck is that banana tree doing in your home?'* Barked Jeppy in the native tongue.

*'Sir the fruit from this tree is only possible through water, sunlight and Christ. I love bananas!'* she proclaimed looking up at the officer.
Joseph rushed over to Geetha and spat into her ear as his hand surrounded her neck:
*'I know who you are, Aappu should keep his mouth shut about you. A sweetheart like you, I can have you gagged, bound and taken into the woods by a few of my friends in town'.*
Geetha could not breathe and yet Officer Rudyard felt it unnecessary to involve himself in a foreign conflict, he did however hear Aappu's name which flustered him. Their horses started to neigh and kick about by the tea shack and so he finally let go of her, causing her to drop to the ground, spitting and coughing for air. Joseph turned and ran in his black shirt towards their horses as he screamed at the little feet that were disappearing into the fields.

The officer placed the book on her lap and followed Joseph. Panchu slowly appeared from the darkness and looked at her friend: her hair was a mess, her skirt was filthy and she was in tears. The dust from her hands left a trail across the cover of the Bible.
*'Joseph, you did not have to do that. You can tell she is Christian, there is no bindi'.*
Jeppy said nothing. This did not stop the officer.
*' Well christ. Looks like you're worse than us Whites',* he joked.
The horses were starting to calm down and vapour from the tea beckoned the men closer for a glass.
*'Well, I have to be sir.'* Said Joseph.

## Chapter Four: Big problems in little Sri Lanka

Just as the tides never cease, life meanders onward. Lekha's puberty ceremony was a blast, the village was decorated with dried betel leaves columned from hut to hut and paper lanterns that drifted from the jungle floor towards the South. Boys danced vigorously in front of a statue of Shiva which was carried through the street as the old men drank their fermentations away. The women surrounded Lekha in colourful sarees as they bathed her in turmeric and sang songs of marriage and motherhood, as to keep her hidden from evil eye. She was physically separated from the hungry men of the village by some thatched leaves, yet they would nevertheless protrude their neck out to catch a glimpse of the girl they spent years calling their little sister.

In the city, Aappu completed the construction of the new ticket buildings and would frequently visit the town concubines with Officer Rudyard and the inferior - Officer McShea. Aappu was given a nickel for tea and would squat by the dusty street side as parts of the opposing shack shook. Once the officers were done, Aappu pulled them by their arms to the closest temple to bathe them and pray for their sins. He cemented sacred ash on their foreheads even though Officer Ellis always wiped his off; Officer Rudyard on the other hand found this all amusing and ironic which infuriated Jeppy who was situated near the construction site. In the subsequent weeks, when Geetha was to give birth; the Governer of British Ceylon - Sir Reginald Edward Stubbs ordered most of his officers to move post, into India. The good workers were to be forced from the Capital across the Palk to the subcontinent to build the railroads in Chennai.

In Kandaa, Panchu had already taken a dowry from an old farmer whom could not find a bride. A couple of cows, a dozen goats and an eighth of his field; was the grand price for Lekha's hand in marriage. When her fiancé entered her hut in a sarong and a metal plate of fruit, Lekha ran over to Geetha's residence for help only to realise she was alone, for her ever-so-helpful aunt was in the presence of the Manasa goddess statue. Praying, for once.

Officer Rudyard's higher ups kept him from sending Aappu home who skipped around the colonial buildings of Jaffna thinking that he would meet his new baby soon. When Aappu skipped into the government office asking for his salary, a reluctant, prickly Rudyard slapped him to the ground. Finally the jovial smile Aappu was known for, had disappeared.
*'You're coming with us to India,'* said the good Officer as he hid his guilt.

Thirteen kilometers away, the candles were set, the drums tuned and the women were buying pigment for Lekha's wedding. Yet Geetha is rushed home by Panchu as she goes into labour.

## Chapter Five


The women of the Kanda gathered in Geetha's hut, it was cooler inside. Colourful cloth unravelled from the midwives' sarees, walled the sweaty, panting Geetha. Children ran to the wells for water but were kept outside by the older men who had decided that this was a good time to stop drinking. Aappu was squatted, crying against the wall of the ticket office that he had built, his colleagues were in the same position. As the officers entered and exited with pieces of paper floating in the wind of their stride, Aappu noticed officer Rudyard sat in the ticket managers' room with a bottle of scotch. *"What the fuck are you looking at!"* Spat a young officer into his face. This resulted in a devilish stare from Rudyard's direction. The humble Aappu kept his head low. He questioned himself as to why he was not able to consummate a child for this long? And why fates twisted existence would ruin his chances of ever meeting his child, or even his wife; ever?

*"I need him,"* she shrieked.
*"Keep pushing!,"* directed Panchu who was in a trance, doing only what was needed for a safe birth.
Lekha was in her hut, dressed in a bright red saree and golden jewels gifted by her uncle. Upon hearing the screams from across the road, she ran out against the wishes of tradition forming a trail from the saree dragging against the dust on the road.
*"I pushed out three of them and you are having trouble with this?"* shouted Panchu above the deafening screams.

Geetha was in a painful frenzy, screaming and cursing. She fought everyone around her but was not able to fight the pain. The hut began to shake but Panchu held her down and split her legs wide open.

*"You fucking bitch, you fat sack of shit. It's a shit for you; it just pops out for you. Look at me! I can't do it. I can't,"* erupted a kicking and slapping Geetha.

Panchu reacted with a smile and placed her hand on Geetha's forehead:

*"Yes you can sweetheart."*

Geetha could ever so faintly see the outline of Lekha in her wedding attire through the cloth of a purple saree and that exact point was when the baby released Geetha from its fury. The entire room sighed and Geetha fell back, warm air expelled from her lungs. The child was born at half past three in the afternoon, just as the construction workers were herded into carriages to be transported across the Strait. This was also the exact time that Aappu slipped away from the guards and ran like a bolt through Jaffna's city streets. He darted past alleyways and shops up the main road and then started using his knowledge of the city. He ran into mosques and temples to exit into the farming fields. And yet he only found his escape through St Mary's Church.

The exit led him into the rice paddies from whence he ran for the tree line as vicious searchdogs bled through the streets like an infection. It was a pathetic escape with no plan but emotion is a plan in and of itself.

In Kandaa the women stared at the dead baby. Geetha had passed out and no one wanted to cut the umbilical cord.

*"An attack on the gods!"* Cried one of them.

*"She is a demon!"* Yelled another.

*"A child as a mother. We should burn her in the presence of Shiva!"* Lekha ran into the hut wielding the same sickle sword that her mother had been threatened with. She reached for the dead child with anger perforating off of her. She sliced once and then covered the baby in her blood red saree. The midwives' were speechless; in this silence a drunken grandfather expelled his wisdom on the issue:

*"Manasa always pays back."*
The limp, bloodless umbilical cord had been severed and Lekha was covered in the saree cloth wall by the wives because her skin was exposed. And thus, she was violently pushed back home by her furious mother. She cried, screamed and then fell as the trees did in the howling wind, to the ground. Her skin visible to the village again. *"You're fucking killing me girl. Get into the hut and stay there like a good bride!"* Begged her mother as she grabbed a handful of her daughter's hair and yanked the weeping bride off of the yellow earth. Behind her, the women of the village spilled out of Geetha's hut and ran straight down the dusty trail towards the Manasa statue but the old Kuravar just watched the passing line of people, shaking his head.

Outside, the birds were still chirping their evening songs, the tadpoles were still calling puddles their home and the red sun was still to pass the skies  but in the hut Geetha was waking up to a blood dried sleeping mat and a dead, blue baby which was missing its limbs. Panchu peered from her hut and saw the Kuravar slowly walking towards Geetha's place. He closed the wooden door behind him which made Lekha squeal as her mother covered her mouth and lay her down next to her sleeping siblings. The wedding was cancelled, a bad omen was blamed.

 It was pitch black. Aappu dodged the light of a burning torch by planting himself onto a banana tree and had killed a search dog for finding him. An aura of whispers punctured the silence of the forest; they were getting closer and louder. It was chaos in pure darkness, panting would occur to the left of him. It would then stop and resume towards his right or behind him, this made Aappu break down. He fell to his knees and then curled up into a ball, he was tired, too tired to cry. Exhaustion took its place and the ever smiling Aappu submitted himself to the sleeping jungle.
Geetha was hyperventilating again, she was in shock. Her child looked more like a snake; it was blue in colour and was born without its limbs. Even its nose had not developed and looked like two slits instead. She cried and cried as she hugged the baby. She would pick up the resting soul and rock it, her flowing tears fell upon her cold

bodied baby. She could not figure if it was a boy or a girl and fell in and out of consciousness as she realised and forgot what had happened to her and her baby.

As she woke again she noticed movement at the edge of the hut, it was smoke. It danced through the darkness of the hut weaving around beams and dodging pots before running out of the window. The Kuravar cleared his throat before inhaling again; he lit a candle on the floor and stared at Geetha.
*"Never seen one like that before."* He began in the most abrasive of voices. *"It is all blue."*
Geetha broke into tears again as the smoke edged closer to her and the baby.
*"He did not get enough blood,"* he said to himself.
*"I killed a snake, and then Manasa killed..."* She paused. *"He?"*
*"Babies are left by young mothers across the realm, especially where I come from. It's a boy... Was"*, his remark led Geetha's eyes to where he sat. She finally noticed his snow – white beard.
*"Do you eat them?"* she asked.
*"What?"*.
*"Are you going to eat us?"*

## Chapter Six

Aappu woke up to Jeppy and Officer Rudyard staring down at him. The other officers were by the carriages with their rifles at the ready, Aappu prepared for the end. Jeppy reached down for his wooden slippers, almost falling in the process, his eyes were glaring, cheeks red and his nose expelled fumes of hot air. His tongue rolled out. The sole of the Sapel met Aappu's head which pushed him back onto the ground. Jeppy had been waiting for this for a long time; he had felt that his own allegiance to his colonisers was polluted by the well – mannered Aappu.

*"A house ridden by debt, a fake smile for your wife. They make you work till you die. When you're dead they'll take her if you're not good enough,"* whispered Jeppy who still hadn't blinked. *"Then when they leave, the wife will send the babies out to beg in the market and she will be lost to the streets.. These whites..,"* his voice loudened, *"and that's the kind of woman that gave birth to you Aappu. A fucking whore!"*.
Aappu said nothing, he was in pain and just incredibly confused.
*"Boys you want any of this meat?",* yelled Officer Rudyard out to the young Englishmen.
A few of them came and kicked the broken Hindu, who's blood left his mouth and splattered onto the long banana leaves.
*"We can take it from here boys. You can go,"* said Rudyard.

## Chapter Seven: Geetha - The Unvanquished

The village had spent the night praying to the Goddess that they had neglected for so many years. Lekha was transfixed in a corner in her mothers hut, motionless and unwilling to speak.

*"It is okay aunty, a little honour lost is nothing for a farmer. I will still marry her."* Said the bridegroom as he flicked bits of areca nut from his teeth into a pot.

Lekha did not move. She sat by the stove staring into space.

On his way out, the groom loosened his sarong as a sign of fear for the demon that lived adjacent to his in-laws'. As did everyone in town, except for the children who would run up to the door all day daring each other to brush it with a peacock feather.

Geetha was in the same position on the mat. She had cradled her baby several times when she was awake and spoke to it, referring to it as *'Ko'.* The elder kept mosquitoes afar with lemon and cinnamon balms, he swept the floor to keep lizards and thus snakes away from the hut and heated water which he could soak his underwear with. This was placed over Geetha's forehead which helped with her fever but she did not enjoy the smell.

*"Do you know what Kurunchi is?"* asked the rough golden brown Gypsy.

*"The mountain?"*

*"No, the flower."* He scoffed, causing the sea shells and ribbons tied to him to jiggle.

*"I only know of the mountain from the esoteric texts."*

Her legs mustered the strength to sit up. She rocked her baby as if everything were fine.

*" This old Kuravan has seen too many of them. Mountains and flowers, it is all the same little girl. It grows in the Ghats where my people come from, swades of purple decorate the lush green mountain sides. There is no snow up there, it is all green. Green till the Kurunchi bloom. And we leave when they do. I pick one from the blackest of stalks to look at its ocean blue interior. It isn't even purple, its sole reason is to further the Ghats, as do people for gods or a sense of humour for your lover. Since it blooms every 12 years, we explore the regions, spread our habits and languages for just over a decade to be back in time for it to bloom. In 12 years little girl, I will be back here with a bright blue Kurunchi for your daughter. I promise you that."* He vowed as exhaled smoke clouded his departure from the hut.

She was alone with her son and her thoughts. For hours she cradled the baby, several hours later she laughed hysterically and beat her chest as an ape would. Her hair moulded into the floor and parts were stuck by blood. Her eyes stayed intense and she shifted upon any flicker of noise, bringing her baby closer to her. She looked down at it.

*"You're a king. Even the God's wanted you to themselves,".*

Ko lay dead, listening to his mothers sweet voice. She looked down at him and analysed her creation.

*"Your chin is like Aappu's. He is your father. You did not get to meet him but he is nice. He is coming for us. Your father, the smart worker. The whole village said we were too old but like the red earth and pouring rain, we combined to make you. Where are you, Aappu? Aappu? Our chickens roam around with no-one to feed them, our people left me to die in our home. Where are you, my husband? My clothes are blood-ridden and I feel myself drifting. I carried a child inside me for almost ten months, if I lose you too, then what? I can see your prickly kisses, I can.. I can..hear your name in the cockerel cries."*

Geetha's eyes slowly came together as she clutched her baby close to her heart so he could sleep peacefully.

*"Where are you Aappu?".*

Jeppy refused to let Officer Rudyard kill Aappu for misconduct as it went against the sixth commandment. Rudyard reached for his Colt

Government Model and pointed the pistol at Aappu who had been ready all day. Trees encompassed them, the green crowd was the spectator of this death.

*"Sir, just do it away from me. Lord rest his soul."* whispered Joseph as he scuttled away.

Aappu closed his eyes and the world around him continued. Leaves propelled by the wind fluttered around the spectating trees that creaked in unison then quietened themselves preferring silence.

*"Run, son,"* muttered the burly old Cornish officer.

*"What?"*

*"Go home you bastard. Run."* hissed the officer as he pushed the stock of the gun onto Aappu's back. And so he did.

The last time Aappu saw his friend was from a barrage of trees. He saw a stoic official shooting a bullet into the ground before stiffly exiting the tree's shade. Birds took flight from the trees as dandelion seeds floated away from their home. Just below the canopy, Aappu brought his hands together to pray in gratitude to his saviour.

Lights from Kandaa's temple flustered the sleeping birds. Snakes slithered through rice paddies towards their nighttime gatherings. Lekha's wedding was over and at the age of fifteen, she was pushed into her first night with her new husband. He played with her hair and pushed her into bed, the teenager moved not a muscle. When he started to de-robe her she clenched her fist and kept her eyes fixated on the straws of the ceiling. He caressed her body as she remained motionless. She could smell him. She screamed. A scream that spread throughout the entirety of Kandaa, a scream that the village women knew all too well, one of seeing a real demon. Even Geetha, who was burying her Prince, flinched.

*"What kind of daughter do you have!"* Shouted her husband as he flung the hut door from its foundations.

*"She's fine! Look, she is just shy. Right sweetie?"* Suggested Panchu as she growled at her daughter.

Lekha ran. Unconcerned for her exposed breast, she ran to Geetha's hut. The villagers that were sitting with the proud Panchu drinking masala milk, watched in horror as Panchu's honour disintegrated.

*"YOU FUCKING BITCH!"*, began her mother. Before silencing herself to the sight of Geetha who stepped out.

Her husband walked onto her land to drag his wife back but Geetha stood in the way, cloaked in white cloth, with a brush of black ash on her forehead. Lekha was still in her borrowed wedding saree, it contrasted with the white of the mother's cloth, both of which were illuminated from the fires lit by the villagers. Geetha's home had been surrounded and yet the two women stood their ground.

*"Cursed soul, you are a living witch. A pagan! You murder animals, refuse to repent and now look what Manasa has done to you."*
Screamed Panchu from behind the torches of Kandaa.

*"And yet you switch gods depending on circumstance. You get choked to death for praying to a god and you're left to die for not praying to another? What is this?"*, responded the Mother.

Some villagers cried blasphemy, and a few people put their torches down. It was Lekha's husband however that raised his hand at Geetha as she spoke, a thundering clap filtered through the crowd as he fell face-first onto the soil in which Ko slept. A chick waddled past the fallen giant. Geetha reopened her eyes to see a bloodied Aappu wielding a metal pot. Their eyes did not meet, for an embrace would come soon, this was not the time for one. The three of them stood against the village, a caged bird, a forgotten soul and a grieving mother.

Panchu cried out to the gods, kicking the dust up to the night, shouting:

*"Your husband is on the floor. What the hell are people going to say? If you ever come home, I will slice you up myself and feed you to the dogs or to that Kuravar whom the witch kept in her house. Teaching her all sorts of spells."*
Aappu reacted not.

*"Go and learn something! All that say I am a witch, take your children to school. Let the little girls learn. For how long will honour be their only lesson? Take them to school and I will remain your witch."*
Asserted Geetha to the village.

Panchu's tantrum caused the crowd to diffuse, only her two toddlers and her son-in-law's family were still there. They had to be, the nupital string was still around Lekha's neck.

*"You don't want to leave your mother all alone. Do you?"* asked a failing Panchu.

*"My mother takes care of me,".*

*"Yes I do!"* confirmed a headstrong Geetha.

*"But he has seen your body girl!".*

Geetha spat on the floor before ordering Lekha into her new home. The crowd was gone, yet one could hear Panchu cursing and swearing all night.

*"Are you really a witch?"* Asked Lekha.

*"You need to learn too,"* was her only response.

Aappu just wanted to see his new little baby and so Geetha took him to where Ko rested. Many villagers lost their sleep that night; from Panchu's cries to Aappu's soul-bursting roars. Several times he reached for the sickle sword, which was still stained with blood from the umbilical cord, so that he could massacre the village that left his wife to die. Geetha out-rightly refused. She held him, like a child. With one arm around the back of his head and one around his stomach, she rocked him like a baby as his eyes teared up further. After some time he fell into Geetha's lap succumbing to exhaustion who played with his hair as he slept. She never did sleep that night. She just sat with a distraught Lekha and her sleeping husband looking over at the grave of her deformed baby. Geetha truly was unvanquished.

## Chapter Eight: In the 1930's

It was said that Panchu remained in front of the statue of Shiva. She sat and cried there for a week before her brother took her and the small ones away for good. Across the sea in Chennai, Officer Rudyard was sent on trial since Jeppy informed other officials of Aappu's escape. And so good old Rudyard spent his life in the West African desert, tending to colonies; never seeing nor hearing from his daughter who waited for him along the rough English coast. When the British departed to Chennai, they took everything of worth, including Jeppy's wife; Jeppy stayed in Sri Lanka. Being hated and beaten so ferociously that he spent the second half of his life begging on Sri Lankan street corners and repeating the same phrase: *Praise the Lord.* Eventually an envelope with a healthy cheque and a letter stating that the new ticket offices were completed by a Mr Aappu Naakkar, drifted via a donkey cart into Kandaa. It had been signed off by an Officer named Skip Richard Rudyard. Lekha studied to be a midwife at the same college that Aappu had attended, she took care of Geetha through all of her pregnancies!

As for Geetha and Aappu. Well, they loved all of their six children including Lekha. On one Diwali night they danced together with the village in the middle of a ring of candles, being as loud as can be; they even drowned out the Gods. They were free. All of them. Geetha spun her youngest daughter who fell into an old man's lap. The man reached for his bag under the light of the lanterns, picking out a bright blue flower. He slid it gently behind the toddler's ear which made the little girl smile.

Geetha noticed the Kuravar. Geetha nodded to the man who blessed her with his right hand from a distance. The old traveller disappeared into the jungle as the little girl skipped through the crowd to show her mother the sacred Kurunchi flower.


## Massacre of some Goats

*It is not a lie that I have seen my own son be cast off a cliff by Imperial soldiers. The mass grave of infants by the rocks below had been washed with tears and blood but there were no clothes as they were stripped beforehand. Xian had asked for nothing from the soldiers, just a bowl of rice.*

*What am I to tell his mother?*
*His mother whose conscience were too pleasant for this world.*
*It's..Hell. I would feed my wife the scraps that my son would not want as she slipped into a sweaty, rambling fit. And so, on a damp and hazy night like this; there would be nothing for me to eat.*

*In a previous life, before all of this I was a graduate in agriculture at the only university around here, the one at the base of the mountains. Before the druggy withdrawn animals roamed the streets, they were my friends. We had been flooded with mystifying agents by the West, men frenzied for violence, food and sex as flames itched their glass pipes. I saw the worth it still had. The rich men were able to transport their families overseas in the presence of a multitude of melons. The export trucks followed The Silk Road so as to not stray.*
*Just before that the educated were sent to farms to promote equality; it was our beloved Chairman's idea.*

*We; me, Chi and Xian were once happy in our family bubble.*

My village was a tired settlement sleeping at the edge of a sharp cliff face. As the sun peeked over the one long road which passed through farmyards and small huts, one would awaken to the humbling cliff face etched with bright green vegetation looking over at the goat and drug fields across the street. My home was the plantation first from the right, I had also rented my properties to good families nearby, my monthly payments would come running down the road. We lived in comfort but to the state I was merely a rich peasant.

Around the time when produce from the wheat farmers was to be sold only to the state, our country's population was urged to kill sparrows and flies as the creatures had been a pest to the sacred harvests. So when all the food was sent to the cities, I asked the arriving cadrè what we were to eat, for this I received ten lashes. Over the coming months, the laughter of children and symphonies of bustling businesses had ceased. People at home would hear tractors and the grunts of iron women tending to molten steel by their backyard furnaces.

'In 15 years our economy needs to be as powerful as the US', proclaimed our Chairman.
So to accelerate metal work across our Great Nation, these furnaces were quickly erected with clay. The iron scraps were sold to cadre in exchange for rice but how can the peasants eat if their pots and pans have been smelted?
Then one day on the Year of the Dog, trucks carrying bulldozers peeked over the long road. They parked up in a single column formation in direct view of the cliffs face. Houses were levelled, all of my properties. Gone. Any peasant that was brave enough to scream or scold the cadrè were beaten to the bone. After tending to the beaten, I walked passed the rubble for my last cigarette, I could hear the crackling of a great fire. I lit it by the fire of my burning Opium field as the villagers screamed in pain and sorrow. I just stood and watched the painting, strokes of bright orange and black blemished the moon soaked fields. In the distance, a single dove tree unable to flee is forced to watch the evil of man.

*My village was once a beautiful place, now it cries in the smoke of the furnaces. Some would say the cliff would smile when drenched in the monsoon season, now it listens to the ramblings of withdrawn peasants and dying mothers. Bodies littered the side of our long road covered in bits of soot. The community house fed grains to peasants that hadn't succumbed to the black fumes but the goats behind the house were for the cities.*

*I stopped caring and started eating, a dead tenant of mine had once said to me:*
*'My mother suffered in the Revolution of 1911, she said that bark or clay can be roasted on a fire, it can provide some sort of sustenance. Bark and scrapings of coal also suffice'.*
*Sparrows were killed for sport which created an absence of flies. The number of locusts rose, which ruined wheat crops across the nation. Cadre grew more violent as the food for the cities depleted: peasants were buried alive, injected with salt water and had their tender bones crushed. It was then, when the scraped coal had taken my fingernails, that my loving wife gathered the women of the village into the community house. By dawn, a dozen women and children hung from the ceiling in a brave act of self destruction.*

*Ash blew itself across the land, tens of millions of the darkest souls floated into the next realm.*

*Now I sit by the community building, my son, a bloody mess of guts and muscle. My wife, hanging from the sad cliff face in the nude. Cadre refused to bury deserters. I'm hungry. Where do I go from here? The end cannot be worse than what I have suffered, yet; I don't know what the end is. A thousand gods have pondered and agreed to bestow this intensity of suffering onto man. Why? Theres my story for you fuckers. I'm going to sleep.*

The faceless man had concluded his rambling and the line of dying peasants laughed in response to his tale, all seemed to have lost their way. Before his dying breath was ready, he held back. He had questions and so with his thin stature and the blackness of coal smudged across his teeth and mouth, he grabbed a sharp shoulder blade lying next to him and marched to the goats.

The first goat he killed was too small, blood splattered across his left eye and hands as he worked hard to hold down the squealing creature. The other few goats could not be used either. From the pregnant one he had learnt to cut around the neck until he felt a crunch. This was when he was to rotate the shoulder blade, the head popped off clean. The final goat was a dream, its head lay on the ground, spitting dark red blood.

This man, with a face of blood, ash and soot fit the decapitated head onto his own after pulling out its brain and parts of its skull. Sharp cuts of bone sliced the man's neck as the head took its place on his thin face. Blood gushed down through his hair, the creature's blood mixed with his own and flowed down his neck. He was suffocating. The blood started to clot, it was almost solid. It webbed, crossing itself over through the dark abyss, the red plasma pulsated. It lived.

He walked carefully only over the plasma as he did not want to fall to his death, however he had failed to notice the hole at the centre of the complex. Falling through shadowy growths of blood vine, the colours brightened as he fell further from his starting point. Bright blood pushed him through the new realm and he found himself lying on the face of a black pyramid plummeting through eternity.

Purple lights flashed in the dark of the black abyss, it started to rain. The pyramid of blackness in the expanse of colourful blood rain, colonised by the faceless hybridized being; continued to fall. The eye of the goat manages a blink.

Sitting opposite him, a bearded man, browned by his climate. The rain continued, it flushed down the body of a palm tree that the bearded man sat under.
"God hates us. Why? In infinite suffering, even death may die. Why would he kill my happiness?".
In response to his questions the bearded man smiles. He opens his eyes slowly, his legs remain crossed.

"What happens at the end? I'm standing at the edge of my world, what's the meaning?".
Frustration was growing.
Not resting his smile, the bearded man answers:
'You're alone'.

Malnourished villagers found several dead goats behind the community house. That night they ate meat for the first time in years. The man's old tenant tucked into thin cuts of his landlord and goats cheek. This was when Yasukè opened his eyes with a stern look.

**Sometime in 1580 - Japan.**
Yasukè removes his trusted katana from the tachikake. He slides the cold steel from the hardened wooden koshirae. He stands by the open sliding door with the loose sleeve of his kimono dancing with the wind. His sword glistened amongst the dawning sun. Etched into the opening of the doorway Yasukè contemplated his dream as his talkative dwarf servant swept himself through the withering wheat fields to shout:
'Yasukè, taste battle for once. In the night as we slept, men ravaged our farmyards. Behold Yasukè, beyond that tree stump lies thirty decapitated goats'.
Yasukè ran softly in short steps towards the sleepy cold sun. Passing the cold bark of the cut Maple tree, he lay his concerned eyes upon the massacre of some goats.

## The Girl from Sinaloa.

**Maria**
**Juan Garcia** - Her Cousin
**Margarita** - Her Mother
**Jose Garcia** - Her Father
**Hernandez Perez Garcia** - Her Uncle / Jose's brother.

**1930's - Sinaloa, Mexico.**

*"María, your hermano is here"*, said her teacher.
The little girl scuttled with her four year old feet into her cousin's arms who had knelt down to give her a hug. She threw her drawings at him in excitement to see his reactions to her masterful artwork. Her small, golden face peered up at her cousin. Her hair had been platted by her mother in the morning revealing her small forehead. Her smile widened when she saw family, it populated most of her face. As Juan Garcia flicked through her work she ran in circles, giggling to herself. Her checkered skirt fluttered with the wind which kicked up the blonde dust at the base of the Sierra Madrè mountains.

*"This is beautiful hermana, let's hurry to your father!"* He yelled out to her as his nasal fluids trickled through the stubble above his upper lip. Marìa's teacher leant against the side of the school entrance as Juan rode away with the little girl, the green mountains beckoned the riders closer. The glistening white horse hidden itself in its own dust trail.

Night blanketed the realm as the sun descended into the Pacific. The sky was violet in portions, silhouetted by small birds dancing on the stage of sundown.
By the base of an orange cliff, close to the beginning of the range, the Garcìa household was celebrating.
Warm singing occupied the silent air which meant the birds' songs couldn't. Vihuela, Maracas and a giant harp blessed Josè Garcia's farmstead. His wife Margarita and little Marìa hopped around in circles amongst the dreamy night in front of the Mariachi band.

Juan sat on the guest rocking chair with his gold plated snuff spoon just under his long nose. The cocaine tickled up his nasal passage. His smile widened and his gaze at the band intensified. He was much darker than his uncle, his eyes were rather small; only after a smoke. His goatee grew a habitation of cocaine specks which he did not care to notice. His large ears nudged his Sombrero and thus he adjusted it before joining his aunty for a dance. He picked up his little cousin with his nose still running and eyes still blaring and danced below the purple night.

The Garcia family had dinner under the stars as the singers blessed their long dining table. Josè's mother and Margarita's sisters set the table with cochinita pibil, dried red chillis, chilaquiles, tacos and homemade guacamole.
*"El patron, we haven't eaten well. The rivers have dried you see.."* said the nervous musician.
Josè, before putting food on his plate, threw him some pesos.
*"Feed your wife, silly man,"* he spurted out, breathing deeply to do so.
Maria ran from one end of the table to the other, upon reaching the end at which her mother sat, she gaped her mouth open. Margarita

galloped a spoon of rice into the hungry opening; her little feet scooted over to the other end and Juan was delighted to drop a slice of pepper onto her tongue. Maria's chuckles were heard throughout the table as she ran back and forth. Her father caught her and threw her up in the air:

*'Hey little stinky, nina traviesa'*, he growled through his beard with a smile hidden behind the foliage.

*'PUT ME DOWN PAPA!'* She sniggers and snorts.

Her father guided her to the ground safely and her little uniform disappeared into the lit up house.

In the playroom was her rocking horse, fluffy monkeys, dolls and toy guns passed down from her six older brothers. She pushed the horse's head down and watched it bounce back into the shadows and forth into light from the garden lamp. The monkeys bored her, she pressed down on one of them - its hands collided and began to clap. The monkey's eyelids receded as its hands came together. As the Mariachi music suffocated gradually from the constant rocking and clapping, the little Chica diverted her attention to her dolls. The smallest doll had a half closed eyelid, she pressed down on its chest. Nothing happened. Maria sighed and contemplated at the wall for the slightest of seconds before picking up a machine gun and gunning down the dancing monkey as theatre gun sound effects gravitated from her small being.

In her running and jumping, she had missed her cousin who had just trotted passed the room to check on the little one. Maria, however, noticed his shadow; the bouncing horse carried with it no light - only shade. Juan was in the back garden.

*'MARIA! COME HERE, YOU NEED TO EAT!'* Yelled her mother with a spoonful ready for her.

*'Mama I'm finished!'* she responded, still scouring the depths of the playroom.

*'She will be asleep in a couple minutes, not much energy left.'* Reassured Jose as he slapped a bug from his wrist. They both caught the eye of the other, Margarita smiled from the side of her mouth as Jose used his eyes to do so.

Around the same time, at the reading table just outside of the playroom; Maria had found her new toy. It shined even amongst the mahogany doors and walls of the farmhouse. It was gold plated. She had to use both of her small hands to grasp it as it weighed a tonne. She noticed an opening and peered into a black hole. Just then, the index finger of her right hand slipped from the cold metallic surface, she tried to reaffirm her grip. She clamped her hand onto the protruding part so as to not drop it and her finger pressed down on the trigger. A cataclysmic detonation sounded from the Garcia home to the Sinaloan towns in the valley.

Long tailed Grackle scattered from the nearby trees and fled to the violet strip of light by the sea as the weasels left the Mexican dust for the bushes once again. The music from the Mariachi band was silenced as the wonky eyed doll proclaimed: 'Too quiero Mama'.

Sat between the doll and the fallen toy monkey was a piece of Maria's skull.

## Several hours ago.

The light of the sun pummelled down on all life directly beneath it, shadows were merely truncated versions of the real thing. Hernandez Perez Garcia's household was quiet, wooden and yellow with dust. Little storms had formed overnight as the air picked up the minute bits of soil. Hernandez first heard the car and then he heard the once sleeping birds fluttering off from the threat of noise - he walked over to his porch and stared out at the golden, barren landscape in the valley. He had not seen his brother in a while.

The all-black 1930 Buick with its giant round headlights and obvious shine (even under the built up dust) bounced over the rocks towards the tree that Jose and Hernandez' boys used to swing from. The rope of the swing had become a number of strings gnawed by ravaging coyotes.
He slid his silver cigarette case open and offered his older brother a joint and so both of them sat looking over the arid wasteland of Sinoloa as they puffed their own clouds up towards the burning sun.

*'What was it, fourty percent for us and sixty to them?'* Asked Jose as he exhaled.

'Well hermano, its fourty on the cocaine and thirty on the opium, given that it reaches California. If it gets to Miami, we're laughing.' Replied Hernandez whom looked exactly as Jose would, had he listened to Margarita and shaved his facial hair for their anniversary. 'Those Chinese Mexicans, they don't know..'Jose inhaled.. 'how much is being sent from here. They count it when it gets there, yes?' 'Precisely' responded the younger of the Garcia brothers.

Just then the old radio sounded fuzzy static noises before playing La Cucaracha for the brothers to hear:

'The cockroach, the cockroach
Can't walk anymore
Because it doesn't have, because it's lacking
Marijuana to smoke.
The cockroach has just died,
They are taking it to be buried
Among four buzzards
And a sacristan mouse.

Both brothers hummed along to the lyrics as smoke filtered through Jose's beard.

'Hernandez listen, let's do this. Sail the opium over Golfo De California with Juan and the kids by the coast. I've got some boys with a couple trucks in Baja that I knew from the revolution who can get it to Los Angeles. If we distribute it right, our odds become 50/50 with the Chinese across our market. That's real money. Maybe 40 - 65 million pesos for the year.'

'What about Junior Wong?' questioned Hernandez.

'Hermano fuck that guy, the Chinese are getting booted out of here anyway. Let them go back from where they came', growled the elder.

'But, they own the network.' said the younger as Juan walked through the back door.

Juan passed the Jesus Malverde statue by the radio as he took a sniff from his snuff spoon and turned down the knob on the radio. Both of the greying brothers stared up at Juan who kissed Jose's hand.

He knelt down to below Jose's line of site. The dust cloud from the horse Juan came in on, passed over the porch from behind the house.

*'Meet up with Felicio Wong. Tell him we are ready. Then go and get little Maria from school,'* he ordered Juan.
Before he could respond, Juan's father laughed as he proclaimed: *'big boy now eh? You're going out on business.'*
The youngest of the three men tipped his dusty leather hat and rode away into the day.
The tired day was warming, they stared at the old tree with the stagnant threads of what used to be a swing.
*'Kids eh? They grow up fast,'* contemplated the elder.
*'You want another one hermano?'* asked his younger sibling.
*'Hell no, Margarita is getting tired,'.*
*'You should go see the Mistress in Chihuahua, she is crazy and beautiful,'*
*'But my brother has already fucked her,'* Jose chuckled.
*'Maybe one of your sons too Jose,'* muttered Hernandez.
They both laughed in the shade from the heat.
*'They don't just grow up fast. They change their ways. In the revolution we would kill for a pistol. Now they plate them gold. Have you seen Juan's?'* expressed Hernandez.
*'Not yet.'* Replied Jose as he flicked the end of his marijuana stick into the soil.

**In the Present.**

As dawn broke over the patches of gold east of Guaymas. The animals repopulated the landscape and the mountains returned to watching over the desert. In the backyard, lizards scuttled over Maria's dead body inside the grave dug by her father. Parts of her brain had been dirtied by the soil, she was still in her school uniform. Juan's grave was five metres away, his hat was missing, including his right arm.

Grandma had fury in her eyes but the old woman did not dare to voice it. Margarita was sitting by the door-way staring aimlessly at one of the legs of the deck chair. The food had gone cold and was being eaten by critters.

Jose, the godfather of Juan, gave the band players some pesos to take his nephew's arm to Hernandez. Besides, they owned the gold on the fingers. Their horses rode into the ascending sun; from the gleaming land rose the dirt trail ending at a severed arm on the black mare's saddlebag. The broken old bearded man with raging red in his eyes but contemplation in his heart, grudgingly tipped the dusty leather hat in the direction of the golden rising sun.

And that is how it began, the fourty year feud between the Garcia brothers.

## THE BLACK SAMURAI AND THE PRIEST.

The conclusion to the Yasuke arc.

<u>Key Characters</u>

**Yasuke / The beast.**
A black samurai who was transported to Japan by a priest named Alessandro in 1579.

**Alessandro Valignano.**
An Italian Jesuit priest who did missionary work across Asia - India, including: Macau and Japan. He transported Yasuke from Africa to Japan. He spent his time writing letters and journals. Born in February 1539.

**Muso Gonnosuke.**
A formidable samurai who lived most of his life as a ronin. He is most famous for his duels with the most feared samurai from the Sengoku Jidai period - Miyamoto Musashi. His signature weapons include a pristine, medium sized katana and a bo which would easily break bones. He was a young samurai at the time in which this story takes place.

**The Lady in Red / Indira.**
A mysterious dark skinned woman from India. Her signature weapon is the South Indian sickle sword, its power is unknown in the Japanese world. She is an expert in the ancient South Indian martial art - Kalaripayattu or Kalari. She owns 100 samurai and plans battles

for land and grain. Indira is usually seen wearing a red saree which is stitched to be a kimono also. She has a scar from her forehead to her eye which was formed from a slice by an unknown powerful samurai. She often says this was her hardest duel. It is not uncommon to see her soaked in blood in some battle somewhere.

### Anansi the Spider.

A collection of cosmic matter which can shape-shift into any shape but he/she prefers to be a spider. Anansi has the ability to warp matter, time and space around it, he/she is said to hold all the wisdom in the world according to African mythology. They will only appear in some ethereal plane given that some form of enlightenment has been reached.

### EKO (ee-ko)

A strangely big child with down-syndrome who spends his time playing the flute by a lake in the forest. He lives in Kuro-Umi and steals from fields. Alessandro takes an interest in the boy so that he may convert the child to Christianity.

### The Dark Samurai

A massive samurai who is fully covered in black armour. Countless battles have slightly worn the armour and dried blood is never washed off of the armour. The dark samurai is semi-trained in Kalari which boosts his agility. He wields a whip, lined with miniature sharpened razors which is a Kalari weapon. He is a legend across feudal Japan and may be one of the strongest samurai during this time. He is paid by the Lady In Red.

### Kamo / The Duck

A short, hairy samurai from the mountains of Northern Japan. He is part of Alessandro's seven samurai.

### Sanosuke

A samurai who dresses in a white kimono but no armour. He is part of Alessandro's seven samurai.

### Kubomaru (Kubo)

A medium sized samurai who owns a thin but sharp katana. He is part of Alessandro's seven samurai.

## The Unusual Woman
A daughter born to Oda Nobunaga and a prostitute.

## Kei
A two year old child with curly hair.

## Oda Nobunaga
The most powerful Daimyo who tried to unify all the clans in Japan. He was killed by one of his own generals in 1582.

## Akechi Mitsuhide
A disciple of Oda. Famous in Japanese history for being a traitor, he betrayed Oda Nobunaga and is responsible for his death.

## Toyotomi Hideyoshi
Another disciple of Oda, a formidable warring samurai general.

## Tokugawa Ieyasu (ee-ai-aa-su)
A legendary warring samurai general who hardly ever lost a battle. Unlike Oda, Ieyasu hated Christians with a passion and wanted them out of Japan.

## Key Items

## Katana
A Japanese Samurai sword.

## Tatami
A mat used as flooring material in Japan

## Kabuto

A steel helmet worn by rich samurai. It can sometimes cover the whole face.

## Kemono
A beast.

## Arquebus
An early type of gun supposedly made by the Ottomans in the 15th century. They were introduced to Japan after Jesuits traded them to samurai lords. Clans that hated Christians had little access to this weapon.

## Karuta-Gane (Karuta)
Steel plated armour worn by samurai. Usually worn over a Kimono.

## Kimono
Traditional Japanese garment with low hanging sleeves. The national garment of Japan.

## Jingasa
A round hat worn by samurai. Made from steel not straw.

## Hakama
A japanese skirt worn with armour.

## Saree
Elaborately dyed cloth which is stitched and tied to form this Indian garment.

## Aruvaa
A South Indian sickle sword.

## Smoke Bomb
Used mostly in Ninjutsu. Creates a smoke cloud.

## Gonnosuke's sugar

Increases speed, energy and ferocity for about ten seconds. Gonnosuke makes it himself. We know it contains sugar but the other ingredients are a mystery.

**The Black Samurai and the Priest**

*Chapter One - Senpai is Dead.*

Nijo Castle - Kyoto region on June 21 1582

Yasuke remembered how his leader lay on the wuthering tall grass with his guts sprawled across the land, painting it red. At Nijo castle, the deceased leader's son fought a blood-washed battle to avenge his father, Yasuke ripped through many samurai to quench his lust for revenge. Nobutada, the eldest son of Nobunaga stared at Yasuke who was in the middle of a cloud of dust, flesh and horsehair.
Towards this filthy expanse leapt a scream:
"If you do anything Yasuke, kill the traitor bastard Mitsuhide!" Yelled the dead Daimyo's son.
Yasuke firmed his grip on his trusted katana, watching a samurai he had called his brother run into a wave of a hundred skilled samurai. Behind them were several more waves crashing in on one another. At the base of the attack was Akechi Mitsuhide, the director of the

coup. Oda's crest of Kiri-mon symbols were being waved across the blackened battlefield, indicating the nature of the war, ultimate betrayal.

Yasuke's black skin kept him the cleanest amongst the warring Japanese. His karuta was worn, there were holes in his tatami style chain-mail, his allies were dying and heavily outnumbered. Death called out to him as it always had been, and so he ran after his brother, killing and decapitating the samurai that Mitsuhide had paid-off. His efforts went in vain, as Nobutada was being hacked for sport. His 26 year old head rolled around as it was kicked about by his executioners, his legs and arms were taken as victory tokens. Yasuke barged through many to try and reclaim the honour his house had lost. He was eventually surrounded and beaten to oblivion before being presented to the cunning Mitsuhide.

The samurai that survived were captured and made to kneel before Mitsuhide who did not alight from his horse. A crescent took over part of his thick metal kabuto. One by one the fallen band of samurai, last of the Oda clan, unsheathed their katana and plunged them into themselves, the blade of the katana cracked the ribcage thoroughly and pierced into their beating hearts. Yasuke's blade was kicked from his wield into the dirt, he was further stomped on as he watched the end of a clan. Oda Nobunaga, the great unifier and Oda Nobutada, his fearless son were dead. A drum billowed out over the field of ash and corpses, Yasuke could hear death coming. Japan fell further into misery as the Sengoku Jidai entered its third and bloodiest phase.

Yasuke was stripped, his armour taken. His samurai status was denounced in a formal ritual surrounded by vultures eating fresh meat and peasants combing the fields for jewellery and prized katana. The black samurai had never been anything worthy until he reached Japan. He travelled with priests, had an eye for faith but it was 'the way' that gave him meaning. Perhaps the Rising Son safeguarded Yasuke but not even the Lord could stop an angry samurai. His Japanese name - Yasuke, was taken from him too, being replaced by Kemono. The 25 shaku beastly brute was repeatedly kicked and pushed further from Mitsuhide until he passed the final corpse. He turned to see a levelled castle and fires still burning strong. Tears fell freely from his eyes, leaving salty tracks leading to his mouth. The sun targeted his nude body as it glimmered against the dark fields, it set only when the beast had passed over the horizon.

*Chapter Two -An excerpt from Alessandro Valignano's papers - July 17 1582*

**To the Superior General in Rome and whomever else is concerned,**

*I write to you, so I may explain my absence. Japan is embroiled in a bloody conflict and it seems that the words of God are blanketed by blasts of gunpowder and rumbling drums. My helpers were ambushed by a clan known as Tokugawa, their campaign is one that comes into conflict with the one true faith. They consider Shinto to be the prime faith, and so they made an attempt on my life. Thankfully my wounds have healed in the care of an East Indian woman's samurai. Her wealth in Nagasaki is limitless, even the bathhouse that I script this from is hers; a most pagan establishment but it helps nevertheless.*

*I must apologise to you General for acquiring the economic stronghold that is Nagasaki. Since Father Viela converted the local Daimyo, this town had entered a vacuum of power only determined by the Daimyo's faith in the Lord. In other words, we did not know that he would give us control of this town, but it happened that way. Only by the grace of God. Japan is a hissing teapot with no tea and I* do not wish to be here when it implodes. Even so, we have made our own enemies because of our unwanted power. The clan I mentioned before, its head is a Daimyo named Tokugawa Ieyasu, he massacred a Christian village to punish me; so when members say I have gone mad and that I am in conflict with Christ, they have no understanding of what happens here. Please remember my work on seminaries in India and Macau, try to understand the political climate.

In the time I have not been in correspondence, buckets of blood have stained the countryside. Japan's most powerful Daimyo, a man who the pagans believe has been sent by the God's to unify the country - Oda Nobunaga, has been forced to kill himself. Oda purchased almost all of our arquebus' and was open to multiple religions and races roaming his homeland. Under Oda was an expanse of coalitions, the man probably had a hundred of his own married across Japan to a hundred other clans. His concubines were limitless and so were his political connections. It is as if he had his own horsemen: Toyotoma Hideyoshi, Tokugawa Ieyasu and Akechi Mitsuhide.

Hideyoshi was a peasant who polished Oda's shoes. He is rather thin and prefers a blank white kimono rather than the lavish silks and colours that Ieyasu likes to coat himself in. Ieyasu is a warlord samurai who had won most of the middle lands of Japan, including Edo for Oda. After recalling our ambush, we figured it was Ieyasu's clan members that almost took my life. Akechi Mitsuhide was the third high-ranking samurai. Tokugawa Ieyasu rode out to seize more land for Oda but Akechi turned back and laid siege to Honno-ji Temple where his own leader slept. Akechi forced death upon Oda and burned the temple because the unifier had scolded him at a wedding. Mitsuhide then murdered Oda's son - Nobutada, apparently the African we had traded had perished there too. For at Nijo Castle, Akechi obliterated the handful of loyal samurai with their own army. He had access to the countless guns we had traded and infantries of money-hungry samurai, each with their own sharpened blades. He even fought with Oda's yellow clan sigil held up high.
Believe me when I say, a samurai with a katana can end a life, one with a gun can end a clan.

*So, this is the climate here. Faith is being ignored for their ears are jammed with thick blood and their mouths froth at the sight of revenge and power. I hope you can forgive my absence and not deem it as an offence. All we can do is convert the peasants.*

*Now to the important part:*

**Provisions For Nagasaki:**
*- Oil, 670 barrels.*
*- Arquebus', 13000.*
*- Tree Paper..*
*-...*


## Chapter Three - Yasuke's Dream

The moon crept over the lush mountains that surround Osaka prefecture but in those days it was called the regions of Kawachi, Senshu and Settsu. The temperature had fallen and dragon breath permeated from the jaws of the beast. Yasuke disappeared into a lush pocket of flora by the dusty road. Horses and carriages rolled by at their own pace in the darkness. He stumbled blindly through dense vegetation, pricking his feet as he went along, till he felt some bark. He scraped at the bark till he felt a good bulk of scrapings in his palm. Most of the night was spent scraping and rubbing till it managed a spit of flame. As the fire drew breath, the surroundings illuminated to showcase dark tinges of green. The last thing Yasuke saw was the flicker of Venus before surrendering himself to the realm of dreams at the base of a black Japanese pine.

A purple sky and a vast expanse formed the world of Yasuke's Dream. He was at the bay of an illuminating river, one step by the water created an aura of blue which outlined his movement by imprinting his footprint onto the sand. Floating towards him, a powerfully green lily-pad encapsulating a little baby snoozing. Yasuke reached for the baby and plucked it out of its natural bed. The lily-pad idled away from the shore. The baby was black, its hair was thick and curly like his own; its mouth moved as if it was suckling in its sleep and made tiny wheezing noises. In his dream he was bearded, he also had on a type of kilt made of thread and beads which covered his body. The further he inspected the baby, the more it looked like him.

*'I must be the father.'* He whispers to himself. As he spoke, a thunderous quake shook their existence. Bits of land erupted from the core of his dream and his baby fell out of his arms. Yasuke fumbled his hands and let out a ferocious cry before opening his eyes to find a samurai shaking him in the rain.

The troupe were dressed in muted colours, clearly their armour had been reused, probably picked from corpses. Yasuke did not notice the dried blood on the samurai's chain-mail as rage consumed him. *'Where is my son!'* He spat at the samurai.

*'We don't know!'* Shouted the samurai, *'You're Yasuke. The black samurai, are you not?'*

Yasuke frantically searched for his child as the samurai expressed their astonishment. He spoke of him as if he were a legend. It was then, without warning, that Yasuke let out a thunderous punch to the samurai's jaw. A click was heard, the samurai's bottom jaw hung out on the wet leaves. The troupe were part of the Hojo clan - their flag of blue triangles was held erect by one of the unimportant samurai who stood at the back. Their mission began when Oda died, they were paid to loot his kingdom and call for an army after assessing the situation in Osaka. Essentially, after a life of wearing oversized karuta-gane and cleaning blunt, filthy katana; they were going to be rich from this one job.

Yasuke had already grabbed the fallen samurai's katana before dodging a dirty throwing knife which pierced into the black bark. The foe closest to him unsheathed his samurai hastily and guided the blade to cut Yasuke. The beast dodged to the right before spreading his legs and crouching down. No one saw his blade, it was just movement and shaded skin against the humid forests surrounding Osaka. Blood sprayed out of a hole in the samurai's neck and drenched the surrounding leaves. Two more throwing knives whizzed through the air, one sliced a portion of Yasuke's triceps. This did not halt his movement however; the next samurai saw a ferocious swing and then darkness. His head was cut clean off, Yasuke ceased his crouch to pummel the headless torso into its peers. Yasuke kept his head low once again, ducking a swing of a samurai before slicing through his faulty chain-mail, his stomach opened and guts flung out onto the forest floor.

An old man waddling around the road. He looked to the woods to see Yasuke's purple skin moving like water in the misty morning air. The trees danced to the wind which howled at the sight of two more squirts of spraying blood. The black figure disappeared into the forests and the old man continued on with his day having questioned his eyesight.

*Chapter Four - An excerpt from Alessandro Valignano's Diary : For God's Sake (2) - July 15 1582*

Dear Diary, it has been a while..

On June 23, my troupe reached the dreary little village by dusk. The sea had soaked its wooden shacks and sea-foam circled the settlement. A palisade sheltered the length of the entire village to deter bandits and thieves. They had a pathetic excuse of a samurai who guarded the entrance. He looked as unkempt as one could possibly look. Nevertheless, the poor soul let us into the village which surprisingly had its own square. The ground resembled clay due to the sea breeze, a large wooden hut peered over onto the square casting the only noteworthy shadow in town. We alighted from our horses.

We walked past a shack where an elderly woman was serving Sake to the local peasants and jobless samurai. They did not notice me at first as my cloak was filthy from the journey, it was Gonnosuke's colourful kimono that stole all the attention. His hakama was embroidered with Japanese serpent dragons and images of his signature bo which was cut from polished keyaki hardwood. He carried his bo in a holder to his left. In a sheath on his right, a prized, blindingly shined katana with a slightly bent tip. This sword was said to be forged over a blistering flame for several months by the famed sword-smith Muramasa's young disciple Fujiwara Masazane. A slice from such a sword could slice through bone in such a way that one wouldn't even know that one was falling apart. The peasants were stunned at such craftsmanship, Gonnosuke straightened his back and widened his stance for the town to see. The sun was receding and the villagers turned to me. A pregnant woman in rags realised I was a priest and screamed to her mother in joy.

The dirty guard slid over, attracted by the commotion. He smiled his one tooth at me till his eyes disappeared and kicked away some fishing sticks which covered a platform. He reached for a rusty knob which swung open a latch, earth from the lid slid off the back. He then reached for a rope and yanked it; the sound of frustrated metal pained my ears. Gonnosuke saw it first, a cross emerged atop of the town-house. The tip of the cross refracted the setting sun's blessings onto the square, allowing the thick clay some beauty. The villagers scraped their necks for the thin woven thread which carried their crosses and showed me them with spectacular looks of relief. Gonnosuke translated that they had been waiting for a priest to forgive their sins.

The power of faith is a startling one. These villagers eat a little rice here and a bit of fish there, they use a single cloth to cover their genitals and bathe in the salty sea. Yet the lord accepted them as his children. They drank, fought and fished together but when dawn broke, they would all sit cross legged and pray to the shimmering cross. A Jesuit named Luciano documented his last visit to the settlement. In a dusty book inside the town-house was his note: *'Kuro-umi, a beautiful little village. The shacks are primitive and need reinforcement. The people have been pardoned and forgiven. Take extra care with the deformed boy - March 1580.'*
Gonnosuke later told me that the peasants had gathered onto the coastal rocks when the sun shone from directly above, to whip themselves for their sins till their skin tore. In an attempt to repent, they had been doing this for two years.

That night, under a single candle flame; I repented almost two hundred sins. The line stretched from our guest shack to the ocean. None self-harmed after that night. When it was time to sleep, we would huddle up close to one another; seven samurai and a priest-listening to the whistles of wind slipping through gaps in the wood. There was always a taste of salt in the air and I was always afraid of rolling onto a blade.

Dawn broke over the shacks by the sea. A little cup of tea had been placed next to my head, one leaf nudged the rim of the cup as it floated. I drank the salty boiling water and looked to the numerous faces staring back at me. The entire town watched me drink my tea every morning as the children fiddled with Gonnosuke's elaborate armour. His grunts sent the children darting across the square. The mornings commenced with prayer before the town dissolved into sake. My troupe noticed a small forest that leaned over to the west of the settlement and asked if they could go hunting, I obliged.

I sent Gonnosuke, Sanosuke and Kamo, whom I called the duck, into the woodland. Sanosuke was of the Amago clan or the house of four squares. The young man was merely a child who carried a personality expressed through one stern facial expression. The duck on the other hand came from the Nanbu clan of the North. These men were smaller but tough and resistant to the cold, they were said to be the true descendants of the 'Ezo' who emerged from Tohoku to create 'the way' and form the idea of being a samurai. Muso Gonnosuke, the most experienced samurai in my troupe, sliced through the woodland to create a path. He was then subsequently kept at the back as his thick armour prevented movement whilst the other two fluttered around the forest in their woven kimono. A light whistle kept Kamo from taking another step. A beetle dug itself into the base of a leaf. The whistle wafted past Gonnosuke who raised his shining blade in the direction of a stream. The wind playfully caught the falling leaves to propel them towards the three samurai as they etched closer to the whistle. Several steps further and the whistle lowered its tone to a flute sound. They continued and the songs of the flowing river occupied the silence of the forest. They had surrounded the source - An abnormally large child, completely bald, playing a pine-wood flute by some water passing over a rock. Gonnosuke brought him to me and told me of the peaceful aura in which they found Eko.

Under the boiling wax of a flickering candle, I sat on my knees opposite Eko who sat cross-legged biting down on a satsuma that Gonnosuke had gathered. He was unusual to say the least: he wore a dirty rag in the Mawashi sumo style, his head was the size of a barrel and he was incredibly overweight which had no explanation since he was a peasant orphan. He started to talk:
*'Money or food for grain, I know big fields'.*
His speech sounded slurry and his tongue refused to enter back into his mouth. I had seen children like this before as vassals to Indian pagan gods. These people were said to be strange anomalies created by the Lord for an incomprehensible reason. I better not ponder over such things. Anyway, Eko was different, the most unusual thing about him was his sheer size, the villagers had told me later that he was only nine years old. Yet he towered over most of the people in Kuro-Umi and would certainly outgrow Gonnosuke regardless of his round belly. I told him that money and sustenance waited for those who listened and immediately started to read from John in the holy bible:
*'For God so loved the world, that he gave his only-begotten son..'*
John 3.16
Eko picked himself off from the wooden floor before I could finish and reached for another satsuma which he had hidden in his cloth. I watched dumbfounded as Eko slowly stumbled back through the palisade and into the lush forest with his reluctant tongue. If Gonnosuke had witnessed such disrespect from a peasant, Eko's head would be rolling around the windy sand on the dark, foamy beach.

The days rolled on and the winds died down. My troupe of samurai recouped their strength and spent their days squashing and drying satsuma's under the rising sun. Their plan was to make sugar for combat enhancements, my pleas that the church owned bricks of sugar in Nagasaki fell onto ~~deaf~~ defiant samurai ears. Eko returned from time to time for rice and coin in exchange for his time, the smiling child would trot back into his green domain as soft flute symphonies blew across our pocket of Japanese coast. The surrounding birds would reply to Eko from the treetops in the language of their realm.

As captivating as Kuro-Umi was, with its quiet alcoholics chatting the day away and private residents who hunted the rough coasts; I had to leave. It is in a missionary's life that he carry out services of the Lord anywhere that is required. I could stay in Kuro-Umi forever and build a real church but my duties lay in Nagasaki. So my plan was to depart on that sunny morning with my band of samurai and Eko. This was until the Woman in Red gracefully entered the village in a maroon Indian saree, the large wooden gates descended behind her. Almost thirty rich, brute samurai surrounded her with brandished katana and walked alongside her in wooden sandals.
'Are you Alessandro?', she asked softly.
Duck stood behind me with his hand hovering over his sheath. One of her samurai eyed Gonnosuke's armour. The wind picked up. Eko was by my side. Colourful kimono fluttered in the wind.
'Yes,' I answered.

_Chapter Five: Yasuke's Child_

Yasuke had been travelling for a few days now. His stubble was starting to look more like a beard but his hair kept short. The heavy rain slapped onto sighing tree-tops, trickled down their stalks and sank into the squished earth. His dark, bare feet sank into this mud as he ran past. Folds occupied his forehead as he sank further into the wet forest. The land was uneven and cliff faces shot up into the clouds surrounded by overhanging vines and erect bamboo stalks. Yasuke wore rags which he had found having ambushed a courier for coin. On his person, Yasuke found a bag stitched together from the same cloth he had put on. The bag contained letters and a few coins. One letter was tied to a pouch, Yasuke hastily opened it and discarded the letter onto the sinking forest floor. It wasn't as if he could read Japanese. He stared at the confetti in the sewn pouch, even trying to bite a piece before tying the brown pouch closed, throwing the bag over his shoulder and continuing on with his descent into madness. Drenched earth had almost turned the paper to sludge but one would still have been able to read it:

_'For our daughter's birthday. Feed our neighbours on the special day. Get her some peaches from the market for me and tell her I love her. Here is some coin for everything. Remember to throw confetti on her_

*when everyone is eating. I want her to feel like a princess' - Shonin
Reo*

Yasuke's firewood was found in a cave which overlooked a tree
studded hill, but he decided to camp out in the open due to roaming
cougars. The rain had stopped in the open but raindrops dribbled
onto leaves and twigs at the base of tree stumps. He shuffled around
wet leaves to make a cushioned platform on which he could rest. It
did not work. He tried to rest, looking up at the engulfing canopy he
repeated the same phrase:
*'My son. My son. My son.'*
Every five minutes he would pinch himself to see if he was dreaming.
He wasn't.
*'My son. My son. My son.'*
His eyes were wide open and refused to blink. The surface of his eye
was flooding with salt water, blood vessels in his eyes strengthened
and intensified their red hue. His eyelid twitched but just would not
blink.
*'My son. My s…'*
Yasuke stopped breathing. Water resting on the canopy was thrown
onto the beast below by a rogue breeze. He pinched himself again
before finally blinking.

The pinch hurt his soft skin which shone under the candlelight. Koki,
his dwarf servant, slept next to him on the tatami flooring. A
silhouette resembling a floating crane drifted by the sliding door of
Yasuke's residence which Oda had provided. The black samurai
jolted up and kicked Koki's bottom which woke him.
*'Get the fuck out!'* He spat at the dwarf.
*'Again? Seriously?'* Replied a sighing Koki as he crawled into the
next room.
Light wood encompassed the interior of the hut and a wood-fire
burned at the centre of the room. Yasuke pressed his fingers onto
the oily, flaming thread of the candle just as the fusuma slid open.
The wood crackled in the background and stayed bright red in the
darkness of the residence.
*'This is no dream,'* Yasuke thought to himself, *'this is a memory'.*
She lay along the side of him and rested her hand on his bare chest.

A hidden woman of the Oda clan. She came from her poor mother, Oda's twelfth concubine whom sexually entertained the local samurai. Her resemblance to Oda was noticeable but her clan would never acknowledge it. She, like her mother was offered to samurai in the House of Oda as an item of pleasure but could not bear a child and so was deemed very 'useful'. Of all the men that had taken her to bed, it was Yasuke that made her feel something other than sorrow. She slipped off her kimono to reveal her bruised body and mounted the black samurai. Not a word was spoken but sweat dripped from one to another as they rolled across the floor naked. The room shook, Yasuke covered her mouth as her squeaks permeated throughout the night. A plethora of black and pale skin contorted around the tatami floor. She strained… Then kissed Yasuke on his uncreased forehead before her kimono engulfed her shoulders and tied themselves around her breasts. Yasuke lay there exhausted. She picked at the burning wooden log with a rod and used a piece to light Yasuke's overhead candle and slipped out of the opened sliding door. The door slid back into place. Koki crawled back into the room and lay down next to Yasuke as the black samurai smiled himself to sleep.

In his subsequent dream he was carrying his baby up a large rock which protruded from the dry yellow earth. He remembered the cracked land, wide skies and shimmering, dusky sun. He was back home. His baby slept in the cloth which was tied around him. The sky was turning from purple to pink and glowing specks from this ethereal realm swam by the ascending Yasuke. He was glad to finally meet his baby properly and was to do so at the overlooking rock. So he climbed up as creatures of his home followed him with every step. Lions and hyena stared him down as he struggled with the incline. Vibrant birds circled their ascension below the pink, milky sky.

From a crevice in front of Yasuke leapt an amalgam of dark matter. It was the size of a dog and resembled a spider with an East -African mask as a face.

'How did you get here boy, you have come a long way?' Asked the anomaly.

Its legs moved and twisted in illogical directions and its limbs were not hinged. It did not look three dimensional, it lay flat on a plane of existence unknown to ours.

'I came to get my son.' Came a quiet mutter. Yasuke didn't understand why he wasn't confused.

'That isn't your son. Didn't he tell you that you must go through this alone?' retorted the anomaly in a rude manner.

'Who? What do you mean?' Questioned the samurai.

'Come, sit with me.' Beckoned the spider in a lower tone.

They sat at the edge of the rock. The skies began to dance with an abundance of colours: greens, blues and shades of red. The lights were bright and danced above the horizon, taking up most of the sky. Yasuke held his baby in front of him who was still in a deep snooze. The anomaly watched his son sleep and smiled in its own cosmic way. The dog-sized mixture of blackness conjured into existence, a tiny urn.

'This is wisdom. I want you to have it.' It said,

Yasuke looked over at it.

'Do you want it?'

'What is it?' Questioned Yasuke as he rocked his baby amongst this foreign, celestial realm.

'Loss. Wisdom's only origin.' Replied the spider.

A loud bang erupted from the urn and blinded Yasuke. Awoken to rocks pelting his face, he exploded in a deafening roar and lay his reddened eyes upon the rain-soaked village from which the stones came. Several villagers laughed and continued to throw them. Yasuke looked at his empty arms. His son wasn't there. And so he looked to his side. His rusty katana was there.

This led to the slaughter of the entire population of Kepu - a small town at the base of Mount Koya.

We were on the roof of the shack looking over the coastal village. It was quite a tranquil day and the waves kept their distance. I watched my step but the Woman in Red walked with confidence across the soaking planks of wood.

*'This cross is no good,'* I said as I pointed to the shining cross which stood erect atop of the shack. Two straight katana were welded together to form a cross, this was blasphemy to the Lord. Violence has no space in Christianity.

*'Don't be so righteous. Its perfect.'* She replied as I wrapped my hand around the cold-steel cross.

I ordered Gonnosuke, who was standing in the square organising a duel with a samurai from the woman's troupe; to polish some wood, nail it together and situate it onto the roof. He complied.


*'I've seen you before on the missionary ship.'* I remarked as I recalled her.

*'I remember, you were with an African that wouldn't stop staring.'* She retorted with no hesitation.

A healed scar ran the length of her forehead to her right eye. This eye was quite milky but it did not feel as though she had a visual impairment, as her movement and grace dismissed that notion. Her hair was jet-black, and she sported a red bindi from India on her scarred forehead. Her outfit was an amalgam of a kimono and a saree; for both are cloth woven into cultural apparel. The saree was dark red which she told me a few nights ago, symbolises blood and fury. Frankly put, she was beautiful.

*'Yes, the African. I took him through adolescence. He was later named Yasuke and became a samurai. Last I heard was that he was killed along with Oda Nobunaga.'*
I said this in the coldest manner, but she squinted her eyes and pierced me with her sight in order to reveal my emotions.
*'You're telling me, that kid I saw was Yasuke? That was 'The Black One' who gained samurai status without being born into it. The one who was given Nobunaga's shortened - prized katana? The one that sat at Oda's table, then ate with him and his family?'* Her voice grew louder and unmanaged. I turned to her with a look of confusion: *'Yes?'*.
The light of the katana-cross struck her dark skin, it made her skin glow.
*'Alessandro, there are not many men that my troupe fear. They will never admit it for their pride is paramount but The Black Samurai genuinely scares them. He is said to be raised as a demon in lands of heat and toxic vapour. It's just funny that you raised him.'* She giggled.
This annoyed me greatly. I could see Gonnosuke return with wood below me.

*'What is it that you want woman?'*
*'It is Indira.'*
*'What?'*
*'The name is Indira. Use it'*
Gonnosuke reached the roof with his polished wooden planks and walked past us.
*'How much for that one?'* She questioned with an eyebrow raised as she peered over at Gonnosuke's extravagant armour.
*'He's not for sale.'* I responded in haste.
My samurai grunted as he worked to dislodge the shining blades.

*'Why not? I have coin. He is just a samurai.'* She searched her
person for a coin pouch.
*'Indira. He is a ronin. He does not work for anyone. He barely works
for me! And certainly won't be in your troupe. We're like friends.'*
I was tense and my samurai's nose flared up. His thick moustache
was twitching.
*'You pay him right?'* She questioned.
I nodded.
*'Some friendship'.* She scoffed.

One of my seven samurai named Kubomaru took Gonnosuke's place
in the duel which was to take place on the square. Knives were
sharpened, hair was tied back and a kabuto was fastened. Kubo
sported a gorgeously woven white kimono with sleeves that opened
to the floor, a polished wooden sheath with a small but powerful
katana. Indira's samurai was covered in armour: his face was
covered by a black mask, his padded skirt was also black and his
kabuto was steel with strokes of dried blood adding some colour to
this dark samurai. His sword was enormous, (fitting for his size) and
bent back slightly near the tip. It had quotes engraved into its matt
portions and the handle was gold.

*'There was a woman, born to Oda Nobunaga and an Oiran. She is
quite slow and unusual, I need you to bring her to me.'* said Indira as
her black hair flowed through the wind.
*'Get her yourself.'* Was my reply.
*'Alessandro, don't be funny with me. Can I march with a hundred
samurai into Osaka? Nearby Daimyo have sent their armies of
thousands to Oda's ancestral home to plunder the family's wealth.
I'm certain that at least three wars are taking place as we speak. So
don't be fucking funny with me!'* She howled, her jaw was clenched.
Gonnosuke stepped forward before I blocked his path with my arm.
*'An innocent priest with his troupe will pass by wars with little
opposition, my army is miniature. I won't stand a chance.'* She
continued. Knowing all I do about her now, it was unusual that she
sounded so desperate.
*'What do you need with her?'* I questioned.

Indira smirked disrespectfully, before spurting out *'see if you were a samurai, you would just do it. You would take the coin and just go..'*
*'I am not a samurai. I am a priest.'*
She sighed heavily, looking over at the calm sea. She reached into her sleeve and scratched her forearm.
*'Look Alessandro, Oda's family is being wiped out. Babies are being massacred because some idiot tells another idiot that the child holds Oda's blood. Let me save this girl from such a fate.'*
A great sob story. It was evident to me that she cared not for the welfare of that girl but was interested in the political power she would inhibit; that is what made her so desperate. Power is money which in itself is more samurai. More samurai give you more land.

On the square below, Kubo lunged at the dark samurai. Kubo's katana was like a needle, it reached towards his neck and connected perfectly by his oesophagus. Nothing happened. The woman in red smiled from the roof with the sun behind her. The needle failed to pierce through the dark samurai's impeccable steel armour. Kubo's foe unsheathed his giant katana and took on the stance - Seigan no Kamae, with the blade facing the sky in front of him. He smacked down the katana once, Kubo blocked. The colliding steel expelled sparks and a deafening noise which bothered Eko in the forest. The dark samurai, raised his sword once again, this time he jumped and struck down again and again with a greater force each time. He smacked the blade down so hard that Kubo's bent leg snapped from the shear force. He fell to the ground. My samurai sat back onto the ground, retied his hair, bowed over as he whispered the lord's prayer and quickly jabbed his needle into his heart. The enormous animal of a samurai took Kubo's clothing for cloth. We buried him that night as I sang hymns from the bible over his lifeless body. This is Japan, this is normal here.

I was lying with my six samurai thinking about Indira. She left India for some reason, made it all the way to Nagasaki and started to pay useless samurai. They obviously took her money and attempted to leave, she kept control with her feared sickle swords. Aruvaa, they're called. She disliked the lack of movement from samurai and the signature neck and armpit attacks, instead deciding to teach them fighting techniques from the South of India. Kalari, I think it was called. Now her samurai leap, skip, twist and use razor whips. Not one of my samurai possessed the skill to take hers on. Then why was she afraid of Yasuke? He can't even fight. Anyhow, I took payment from her, put some money aside to rebuild the settlement and went to sleep...

A noise woke me before dawn. It was an old man who wanted to watch me drink my tea. There was no tea. He stared at me, looked to my left and dropped his jaw to the ground. I was still rubbing my eyes when he gathered the entire village, they rushed in and started to kick and punch me. Two naked women were escorted out of our shack and thrown onto the clay ground. They had successfully separated me from my samurai and I felt feet smack my face. A samurai from the settlement threw me down next to the women who received a similar beating. The old man stated that he had seen the prostitutes caress me and that I was a fake prophet. I had been set up. Chaos showed its face: people threw wooden slippers, spat on me, kicked me repeatedly. I sat in the middle of the square, praying to the new wooden cross. People were screaming, children cried and the cross started to burn. This hurt me the most. Why?

Eko ran towards me - trying to throw people off of me. Certainly I was to die here. The quiet settlement by the coast was the loudest in Japan. Eko was thrown to one side, at this point my robe was covered in mud and the cross around my neck was ripped off of me. A samurai beheaded both of the women, and I was next. Shacks behind me were on fire and one of my samurai was overwhelmed and murdered. Just then, Gonnosuke rode in on his horse waving his polished katana and bo through the crowd. It was a massacre. This created an opening for Indira to ride her horse through bodies. She bent from her horse in an inhumane manner, her face was near the horses hooves, but she was able to lift me in one swoop. I was now on the back of her horse somehow. I could see Gonnosuke just hacking away at villagers.
'That's why I wanted to buy him!' She screamed as she cackled to herself. Indira is clearly crazy. At least we were safe. She rode to the palisade and opened the gate.

On the darkest night, the burning town gave us light. We rode out. I heard it first, a distant horn bellowed through the black night. Drums were being beaten, it sounded as if it came from the clouds. It was then, that very moment; Indira spotted an army of a thousand samurai sprinting across the same road I had come from.

*'We're dead.'* She whispered. Indira rode back into the town and told everyone to run for their lives, for death was imminent. When one's faith is obliterated, the ensuing rage is deafening and so no one listened.

*'Watch it!'* Screamed Gonnosuke, still fending the locals away from him. A blanket of arrows fell onto the settlement. Another one of my samurai took an arrow to his pupil and died. Indira's samurai left the massacre inside the settlement and ran out to the gate.

There we stood, thirty kalari-samurai, the duck, my other two samurai, Gonnosuke and the Woman in Red. Just watching. Hundreds of hungry samurai spill across the land screaming. The drums did not go any quieter and horses were kicking up the thick mud. Was there any point in praying? Each and every person on that front was sweating. People were twitching. It was helpless.

Amidst our silence, Gonnosuke roared and gripped his sheathed katana before running out onto the field alone. For that, I will always respect that legendary ronin. The others followed, just screaming. A war is a loud place. Indira rode out to the woods to the left, leaving me by a tree stump. The armies met with a loud crash, bodies flew over others. From my vantage point it was clearly a Tokugawa army, the general at the base of the attack carried the crest of three leaves. He was likely informed by his leader, Tokugawa Ieyasu, to start to rid Japan of Christianity following the death of Oda. So in a way, this was all my fault.

The first wave of opposing samurai was obliterated by kalari-techniques, Indira's samurai would dodge cuts to kill with one slice. The dark samurai smacked down his whip in front of him. This extended it by five metres, following this he span it all around him. Skin was being ripped from the opposition, bits of flesh were flying across the battlefield. Blood splashed all over the dark samurai who was roaring and spinning in the middle. Gonnosuke blocked a slice and split his legs wide, he cleaved downwards with unmatched force. One samurai was cut cleanly in half. Another two blades flew towards his face, he dodged one but the other slice took a chunk off of his kabuto. He drew his prized katana closer to his stomach and waited a moment. The opposing samurai aligned for another attack but Gonnosuke stepped forward plunging his katana through both men in one go.

The woman in red rode to the battlefield from the forest. From her back she equipped two sickle swords with rusty wooden handles and spun them from her wrists. The opposition did not even see her coming from the left when she started hacking at them. With the spin of the sickles and the force of her horse, bits of tongue, eye and bone splattered everywhere. Men amongst the Tokugawa army started to throw up at this site. Indira's samurai watched her screaming and laughing whilst riding through a population of samurai on her trail of eradication. They followed her on foot, stabbing any samurai that missed her sword. It was truly disgusting. The dead were emptying their bowels from the intense circumstances from which they died.

Many of our own were dying. The duck stabbed and sliced upwards, holding his katana over him as he finished them off one by one. Five samurai surrounded him, he slit the necks of two of them before the third cut upwards into the duck's armpit. They ravaged his dead body like animals and carried his corpse away. Blood flowed through the battlefield as if it were all one organism.

Hundreds were dead, most of Indira's samurai had perished. It was Sanosuke, Gonnosuke, the dark samurai and a few others that were left. But they were slowly being surrounded. Sanosuke brushed his white kimono, Gonnosuke equipped his signature bo, the dark samurai reached for his giant katana, Indira was still creating pools of blood further up the battlefield, and I was spotted by some villagers. An arrow pierced Gonnosuke's armour, his arm started to bleed profusely. Another arrow flew towards them, Sanosuke unsheathed and sliced it mid-air. He looked heavenly in his bright white kimono as the sun was awakening. More and more samurai circled the three samurai. I ran towards the battlefield, away from an angry mob.

Indira positioned herself directly in front of the general. She kicked her horse twice, made two click noises with her mouth and her horse shot forward, throwing men to either side of her stride. The general spotted her and reached for his bow, Indira lifted her legs up and squatted on the horse's back. The general released an arrow which skimmed the horse's leg. She etched closer amongst a pit of a hundred samurai. He released another which pierced her horse's front thigh. It falls face first onto a couple samurai but Indira leapt from this momentum. The last thing the general saw was an angry Indian woman coming down on him with a blood-stained sickle.

Gonnosuke was cracking skulls and breaking bones with his bo whilst the dark samurai sliced limbs off of samurai who were coming too close. This is when he spotted me running in from the forest. He barged through a wall of katana like a ram to reach me, Sanosuke used this as an opening and sliced elegantly when he noticed a protruding limb. He wasn't as lucky as Gonnosuke though. Bathed in blood, Indira appeared to the right of Gonnosuke, she was truly in red.. She threw a katana to me and pointed to the burning shack in the village. I could faintly see something. I squinted my eyes. Eko had been crucified onto the burning cross. I started to cry. My faith had finally been broken.

Gonnosuke forbade me the sight of Eko's struggle. He reached for a bloody yumi on the soil and whistled for his horse. The villagers had almost reached us, arrows flew past us and another wave was running towards us. An arrow pierced my thigh and I fell to the floor. Gonnosuke slowed his breathing and widened his stance; the horse was arriving. Death was nearing. He held the yumi above his head and followed the ancient techniques taught in kyeudo schools. Gonnosuke paused his breath and released his fingers from the anchor point before throwing me, Indira and himself onto his horse. He did not look to see where the arrow went because he already knew how it would bend and spin before cracking Eko's skull. It pierced through the entirety of his brain, splitting the wood he was crucified on. The boy was put out of his misery.

Indira signalled for another one of her horses as we rode away from death. Arrows zapped past our horse and hundreds of samurai roared for their general. It was haunting. A beautiful brown horse joined our ride, it galloped along the side unafraid of commotion. *'Gonnosuke, ride out to Osaka. Find her for me.'* Shouted Indira amongst the deafening sounds of demise before slipping him a note. Gonnosuke turned and looked at me. I nodded to him. Indira reached for the other horse and fell onto its back. Gonnosuke pushed me to her. We rode towards Portuguese Nagasaki, where I am now.

As I rode away from the burning village by the coast, the sun had risen up from the horizon and was peering at the countless dead. The horse was dripping blood from Indira's soaked saree. She smelt like metal. The dark samurai's power and skill was admired by the Tokugawa clan who took him in. My whole troupe was dead, the rest of Indira's men were all dead. She had only sixty left in Nagasaki. The entire village had drowned in fire and it seemed like no one had survived the onslaught. Eko was a pile of ash somewhere in the square. The flora surrounding the settlement was watered with blood that morning. As I watched Gonnosuke disappear away from the sun into the heart of the Sengoku Jidai. I couldn't help but blame myself for all of this.

*Chapter Seven - Yasuke: The Black Samurai*

The baby was still asleep, with its little fingers wrapped around his fathers pinky.

*'Oh you're back.'* Said the anomaly.

*'Yes, sorry I was troubled and woken. It won't happen again.'* Replied the black samurai.

It was an unusual realm that changed seasons every couple of minutes. The leaves on trees would repeatedly grow into lush water-filled green specimens before wilting and losing their colour. The browned leaf would be disowned by the tree just as a new one grew. This left many dying leaves floating in the wind under the colourful sky.

*' Who are you anyway?'* Questioned the Samurai as he stood up to stretch his legs. The beads on his outfit contorted with the movement of his body.

The mask on the 'thing' shifted, the mouthpiece did not move though: *'I have quite a few names, people call me the trickster, Kompa Nanzi or just Anans…'*

The cosmic entity silenced itself as the sky clapped like it would when populated by violent storm clouds. A giant cloud split in half as the ground shook around them, a pink aura seeped through the water of the clouds.

*'Yasuke, take this wisdom from me or else you will perish.'* Insisted the trickster.
The black samurai in his tribal attire reached for the urn once again, as if pre-determined to do so.

The baby was asleep on his lap. The enigma stretched all eight of its cosmic legs. The matter around each of its dark legs would bend and warp the surrounding space, as if it were absorbing the reality around it. The light from the sky had now reached Yasuke and the trickster. The pink aura stroked Yasuke's face, the trickster bowed his mask and finally he opened the urn. Sparkles inhabited the space around them, a plethora of colours shifted and bent itself like a thousand snakes. Yasuke felt himself float off of his feet, the shine was brighter and almost blinding. Leaves circled him, his consciousness warped as his black skin started to peel away from him. He was disintegrating and rising towards the clouds. Behind him, along with the anomaly, was his mother peering out from the rock holding the wisdom of loss all those years ago. Knowing her son was lost forever. She was crying.

By a transit village - Gokurabas, in the surrounding misty rainforests of Koya. He awakened. Yasuke - The Black Samurai defeated his mania and climbed the mountain to find the woman he loved. It didn't matter that he was losing his mind, she would not stop attracting him from across Japan. And so, like a moth to a flame - he ran through the dense jungle towards the little light left in his dark life. He thought of his life as a samurai in Japan, how there was little honour in *'the way'* and all the people he had massacred. He hated himself. He figured that his woman had no hate for him and that was enough.

The climb was hectic, the mountain shook in its showers. Nearby monasteries were set alight by bandits who were looting Oda Nobunaga's property. Yasuke stopped to catch his breath, he surveyed the region from the mountainside. Pockets of red dotted the moonlit ragged forests, screams flared out of these dots of red before drowning out from the wails of down-sloped winds. He turned around and continued his climb till he reached the road of graves.

The trees hung over the little granite rectangles that stood up from the mountain's mossy vegetation. More than two hundred thousand of them. Yasuke waded through death for almost an hour before reaching a shrine known as Kongo Sanmai-In which was surrounded by passing mist and pink roses. Corpses of monks were sprawled out around the shrine. Yasuke stood over one, ripped off the robe from the dead soul and spread it over his own battered body. He shuddered and entered the shrine.

Yasuke spent days searching all the settlements across the mighty Mount Koya. He found only more corpses and signs of looting. From his vantage point, he saw thousands of samurai clashing with thousands of others in the farmlands surrounding the alp. He was squatting, eating grapes when he heard a conversation from the bush behind him.
'How insane! I thought it would have been Tokugawa Ieyasu who made Akechi's head roll!' Said a voice.
'Right? In the end it was Toyotomi, the sandal scraping peasant.' Remarked the other peasant.
'I can't believe it. Fucking Toyotomi Hideyoshi controls most of Japan?'

Yasuke was surprised. His lord had been avenged by the general whom he had least expected. The moment Toyotomi's messengers told him of Oda's death; the sandal-scraper rode out to Yamazaki in Kyoto where Akechi was convincing his families houses to stand with him. They refused since he had betrayed Oda in such a brash way. Ieyasu was riding to the same location with his entire Tokugawa clan of 15,000 samurai. Although, he was several days behind Toyotomi due to matters he had elsewhere. They were all thirsty for revenge. Toyotomi met Akechi Mitsuhide's army in Yamakazi with 13,000 powerful samurai. The betrayer defended himself with 12,000 of his own samurai whom he had stolen from his dead leader. The armies clashed, guns blasted their gunpowder across the battlefield and countless litres of blood drained into the Japanese soil once again. Akechi fled on his horse as a troupe of samurai chased him down. He died at the hands of some very excited samurai in a most violent manner.

In a very remote part of the mountain, Yasuke walked past a shack. He stopped, catching a whiff of something familiar to him. It was her hair. Yasuke composed himself and his beard also, he removed his wooden sandals in front of the shack. He removed his sheath and rested it onto the outside of the shack. He knocked. No answer. He knocked harder. No answer. The door creaked a little from the force of his knock. The floor beneath his feet made rustling noises. He pushed the door to find his lover mutilated on the floor. She had been decimated by a passing group of bandits. Yasuke's hands started to shake and cry. He turned her over to reveal her once beautiful face. It was over. He punched hard into the floor and himself, forcefully attacking himself till his black skin boiled with purple bruises. He thrashed the floor some more, it broke through and a figure moved below.

He roared as he ripped the floor from the shack. Bits of wood flew from Yasuke's palm. His furious eyes shifted direction without meaning, he was falling back into the beast-hood he had just escaped. Phlegm and saliva fell from his mouth as he teared away at the floor. He stopped. His eyes slowed and he wiped his mouth. Under the floorboards, a little hand pushed Yasuke's face back. It was a dark hand. He reached into the hole and felt a bite. For a second he saw her, a little girl no more than two years old nibbling on his hand. Her eyes were oriental but her skin was Yasuke's, her hair curled like his, and she was ferocious like him. He reached in again and picked her out of the hole. Time slowed, the little girl kicked and punched her father as he stared into her dark eyes, smiling. He had fallen in love once again. She was the most beautiful thing he had ever seen. He noticed her fat cheeks which were like his mothers and her button nose, the one she got from her mother. Yasuke cried with happiness as he was beaten by the toddler, his tears fell onto his dead lover.
*'I will protect you forever.'* He said to his child.

The two of them spent some time in the mountains: hunting, playing and making fires. Yasuke flicked through his lover's belongings to find the childs name, he could barely make out what it said:

Yasuke-Kei - was her full name. He put together a usable kimono from an old rag and katana sliced thread; now both father and daughter were matching. They stood at the edge of the hot springs watching smoke billow from perfectly aligned wooden logs. Yasuke gave Kei some incense which he had found, she held them tight with tears filling her big eyes. The little girl's kimono moved to the wind, her small stern face caught Yasuke's attention. He then turned to his lover burning into the summer sun. Yasuke was pleased with his daughter's bravery, he rubbed the little one's hair.

Below the shack, Yasuke had found an indigo bleached kimono in perfect quality. The blue complexion of it was pristine, and perfectly woven. He turned it over to reveal crisp embroidery of a flower. The flower was purple and sort of opened up from its stigmata to express its strong colour. Below the flower, it said 彌助 (Yasuke). When he held up the blue kimono, another identical kimono fell from the inside. It was tiny. That night, Yasuke spread a cloth out onto the broken floor and filled it with everything he would need - coin, clothes and food. He put it to one side and fell asleep with this daughter in his arms. That night he did not dream.

He hadn't really risen from his slumber. He was in deep thought. Kei carried the royal blood of Oda whilst also carrying his own blood. He had to take this little one as far away from Japan as possible and the only way to do that was through Alessandro. He dressed Kei in the blue kimono and prepared for the journey which they were about to embark on, when someone flung the door open, creating an overcast over the black samurai. Gonnosuke stood as tall as the length of the door, his armour was worn but nevertheless glistened in the morning mist.
'Yasuke?' He grunted as he looked down.
Yasuke quickly fell into his kimono and barged the mammoth out onto the moss, grabbing his rusty katana as he did so.
'Not now! Just leave us alone!' Screamed Yasuke cloaked in his dark-blue kimono. His lips quivered and eyebrows dipped into his eyes. He shivered once, the kurinchi flower on his back fluttered as he did so.

*'What the hell are you doing here?'* Yelled Gonnosuke, who had not yet touched his sheath.

*'Nothing. Please just leave. We need to go.'* Begged Yasuke. He was desperate. All the rumours Gonnosuke had heard about Yasuke stood as a lie in front of him. This man was not a fierce brute but a broken little boy.

*'Who is we?'* Questioned Gonnosuke as the black samurai kicked himself.

A creak was heard. Both men peered to the shack where Kei was watching from.

*'Kei! Run!'* Screamed her father as he took stance.

A water droplet on a leaf above a warm pool at the hot spring found it hard to drop off. Through a crazed misunderstanding of love, Yasuke attacked and so, the two legendary samurai faced each other off amongst the cloudy cliffs, burning monasteries and boiling hot-springs. Gonnosuke took on the Jodan-no-Kamae stance, raising his prized katana above his head and spread his legs. Yasuke held his old katana in front of his chest, pointed towards the floor.

*'What is your business with this girl?'* Shouted the brute before dashing forward and bringing the sword down on Yasuke who blocked it by raising his katana upward. Clashing steel pushed out the nearby air. Leaves fluttered. The droplet fell into the hot water, causing a perfect ripple across the water's surface. Gonnosuke unleashed a fury of slices which Yasuke blocked with great effort. A horizontal cut came towards Yasuke's cheek which he ducked before slicing upwards into Gonnosuke's hip. His katana was too blunt to pierce through the brutes armour.

Gonnosuke pushed back the black samurai who fell into thick mud. He then proceeded to reach for the little girl. The details of his mission mattered little, he had to upkeep his honour to Alessandro and Indira. He just needed to bring back this girl from this location and that was that.

*'Please. That is my daughter!'* Yelled Yasuke from the mud.

Gonnosuke pulled the little one's arm. Kei bit the brute and threw a number of punches and kicks. Seeing this, a plague of fury engulfed Yasuke. He shrugged the mud off of the Kurunchi flower on his back and ran towards Gonnosuke who turned at this point. Yasuke plunged in for a stab, the brute dodged it. An upwards cut came from Yasuke's blind-side which the black samurai maneuvered around. This momentum allowed him to thrust himself forward into his powerful right hook which smashed into Gonnosuke's face. The steel mask caved into the brutes face and blood seeped from the openings of his armour. Yasuke did not stop, he pummelled the brute with his fist till his kabuto was punched off.

Gonnosuke coughed blood. His scarred face screwed itself into anger and blood swam through the gaps in his moustache.
*'Get the fuck off of my daughter!'* Spat Yasuke with his eyes glowing red.
The brute scoffed before spitting red onto the moss. He reached for his pouch, opened it and poured sugar down his throat. His eyes widened, he felt a kick and leapt forward. Two slashes came for Yasuke followed by a hit from the brute's prized bo. Yasuke dodged the blade, the bo however, had struck his stomach. This lifted the black samurai off of the ground, from there Gonnosuke grabbed him and threw him into the base of a tree. The ground shuddered and falling leaves drifted slowly in the wind, falling at five centimetres per second.

Gonnosuke dashed toward Yasuke as the hot pools of water smoked in the background. Yasuke raised himself and tried to commit to a stance. The two bodies collided and little Kei started to cry. Gonnosuke dropped his sword and coughed. Blood sprayed profusely from the side of the brute onto wet bark. Yasuke sighed. They were both knelt, face to face. A bloody yumi fell from the back of Gonnosuke. He had run directly into Yasuke's rusty katana. All was silent. The wind picked up again. Gonnosuke reached beneath his chest armour for a soft-cased black ball. He smacked Yasuke across the face with tremendous force.
A black smoke surrounded Yasuke who was still reacting from the slap and encompassed him completely. Gonnosuke was gone. Kei wasn't crying anymore. He could hear a horse galloping away and almost broke down before composing himself. He reached for the Yumi in complete darkness and sat up onto his knees.

Yasuke closed his eyes and prayed for the safety of his child. He sighed a breath which cleaned the smoke closest to his nose and raised the yumi above his head. He kept his eyes closed and listened carefully to the horse's hooves. Yasuke knew about the only horse-trail out of this area of the mountain. His kimono spread out over the moss as he knelt and pulled the string back close to his chin. He took a deep breath. Yasuke released his fingers after a couple of seconds and the arrow penetrated through the smoke, clearing his view. Yasuke picked himself up and stumbled off into the woods with his hands questioning the skies, no longer caring whether he had hit Gonnosuke. Yasuke finally understood the wisdom that had been bestowed upon him. Loss.

The arrow flew up high and dipped over the curvature of the mountain, it spun and screeched before slamming into Gonnosuke's armour. It pierced the chain-mail and dug through the back of his neck and out of the other end. A blood splat landed on Kei's hair but the brute attained his grip.

It is said that Yasuke was last seen somewhere on Mount Koya building a shrine for his lover and her father: Oda Nobunaga. He was never seen again.

*Portuguese Nagasaki - Several Days Later*

Alessandro finishes his writing and comes out to the porch of the bathhouse after hearing a horse galloping towards his proximity. He skips out, with a bandage across his leg. The lady in red joins him, she has a stern look on her face. The salt from the sea sprinkles itself over Portuguese Nagasaki. Gonnosuke's horse reaches the compound and the bloodied samurai falls off his horse directly in front of Alessandro. The lady in red looks up to the horse to see a little curly haired, mixed-raced girl looking back at her, wide eyed. Alessandro instantly realises who the child is and breaks down over Gonnosuke's body. The body is dragged away by Indira's samurai. The lady in red picks Kei up, the little girl spreads her arms around Indira's neck and stares at Alessandro from her back.

*'She looks just like Yasuke.'* Said the broken priest.

The lady in red contemplates the warring state of Japan as she holds gently onto Kei, the daughter of a most legendary samurai.